Eclectic Ensemble

A Random Collection of Short Stories

Bruce Clark Bennett

Contents

(About the Author)

Bruce Clark Bennett is a visual artist by trade but caught the writing bug later in life. Having been fascinated by stories of scientific discovery – both real and imagined – Bruce began conjuring his own tales of wonder and discovery, often inspired by actual events. Character identity rediscovery is also a theme that runs through many of his stories. Bruce invites comments and inquires at https://eclectic-ensemble.com/

ENCELADUS INSPIRATUS

Bruce Bennett-©2020

A majestic view looking downward at the Grand Canyon begins our visual journey as we slowly ascend. Through the clouds, we accelerate faster till the entire Earth is in full view. Rapidly, we fly deeper into space, passing Mars then through the asteroid belt. We fly past Jupiter, with her familiar Great Red Spot slowly spinning, then past her moons, Io, Europa, Ganymede, and Calisto. We turn to deeper space and see a tiny ringed planet directly ahead, getting larger as we approach it rapidly. As we come near, the spectacular rings become more and more defined. Just as we are about to fly right into Saturn, we veer off and fly past several of the inner moons until Enceladus is directly in our sight. As we come closer, our approach slows. We see a complete fly-around of the small planet and observe the detailed, wrinkled surface. As we view its dark side, it is backlit by the sun. Here, we see geyser plumes spraying upwards from the planet. We begin to fly closer and closer to one of the plumes. Just as we are about to fly through it, our direction tilts down toward the emanating geyser, and we dive straight down into a dark trench. As we descend toward it, all fades slowly to black.

***

Al Williams enters his small, disheveled apartment, returning with his mail. As he shuffles through the letters, he is oblivious to the TV in the background droning with the network news. Bill, another bill, overdue bill…until he comes to that all-important letter he has been anxiously awaiting. It is the reply from Ballantine Books about his latest story submitted for publication. He takes a deep breath and closes his eyes as if to say a quick prayer. With a racing heart and sweaty palms, he opens the envelope. He ever so slowly inches up the letter from within the envelope in nervous anticipation.

"Dear Mr. Williams, We regretfully inform you that your novel Secret Labyrinth of Io has not been considered for publication…"

Al sighs painfully and quickly turns away in disgust, not wanting to read further. This is an all too familiar outcome. He flicks the letter away, and it floats to the floor to land with other clutter and debris. On the TV, a science news story describes the discovery of carbon elements within the plumes of Enceladus's cryovolcanoes. Al is too lost in despair to pay attention to news that he otherwise would be very interested in following. Finally, he composes himself and returns to the other letters, hoping for some glimmer of good news. The next one is a royalty check from Ballantine Books. He opens the envelope and examines the check.

"That little? How am I going to pay the bills this month?"

He moves on to the next letter. "Well, what other good news have we here?"

Oh god, it's from his ex-wife's lawyer. "Must've missed child support for another month."

He doesn't even bother to open that one—not until he's had a couple of drinks, anyway.

The next letter has OVERDUE printed on the outside. And yet another letter has FINAL NOTICE on it. He dejectedly tosses all the letters onto an existing pile of unopened envelopes on the cluttered desk. He just stands for a while, sulking, before he shuffles slowly toward the couch. He picks up the rejection letter and plops down to lie on the couch. He takes the publisher's letter out of the envelope and begins to read it in its entirety. The second paragraph really hits at the heart of the matter.

"Allen, we have always honored our relationship with you. However, since your last success, Daedalus Rising, five years ago this summer, your stories have lacked the thrill and enthusiasm necessary to be viable publications for us to consider."

Al closes his eyes, hiding his face with the letter, and begins thinking of better times. He envisions a montage of past moments, starting with the day he got the first shipment of his published book. The family gathered, enjoying the thrilling moment. In his mind, Al reaches into the box to pull out one of the hardcover books and holds it up.

Beaming with pride, he says to the kids, "Look! Daddy has a bestseller!"

The celebrations, the parties, the book signings—it was a wonderful time. In their beautiful, large house, life was idyllic. There was the playful, loving time with his wife, Lorna. Fade to black. Then, the pressure began to do the next novel. The expectations...the writer's block…the impatience with kids and wife. Then, the first rejection notice…despair, anger, blame, arguments…then the drinking. Finally, that painful scene when Lorna leaves with the kids, slamming the door behind her.

He wakes up abruptly, the publisher's letter falling to the floor. He rolls on his side and notices the small whiskey bottle on the coffee table. He can reach it without getting up. Taking a swig, he looks over at the TV, which has been on continuously.

The news announcer: "And tensions continue to worsen in the Middle East. For more on this story, we turn to our foreign affairs correspondent on location..."

CLICK. Al switches over to the Science channel, broadcasting a story on the latest NASA space mission. They are in the middle of a brief historical summary explaining how, in 2014, the Cassini-Huygens spacecraft first discovered the geysers of Enceladus, purporting the presence of underground oceans. Where there's water, there is the potential for life. Now, when the Cassini II launched in 2016 and discovered the carbon traces in the plumes, speculation ran rampant as to the possibility of life existing in the subterranean ocean, six miles beneath the surface.

Al at least has his head off the pillow now, watching with more interest. He turns up the volume.

An interview with a well-known astronomer begins while the crawl line reads, "Science Community Abuzz Over Discovery."

The interviewer asks, "So, is there life at the bottom of the trenches on Enceladus?"

The astronomer replies, "Well, (chuckles) we're not sure, but we are extremely excited that the government space agency has vowed to send a space probe to find out. The notion of other life forms in our solar system is the subject of one of the greatest explorations of our generation".

The scientist describes the proposed mission to Enceladus, showing a computer simulation of how they intend to drop a probe down into one of the trenches of the "tiger stripes," a series of four trenches on the planet's South Pole that looks like a huge claw-scratch on the surface. When Enceladus's orbit is closer to Saturn, the trenches emit the plumes. When the orbit is furthest from Saturn, the geysers subside. It will be at this point that they will deploy the probe.

Al is now sitting up and watching with full attention. He swipes away clutter from the coffee table so he can find a legal pad and starts writing notes. Occasionally, he glances up to see the visuals regarding the planned Enceladus mission as he continues to jot down facts from the program.

As the TV segment comes to a close, Al gets up from the couch, waves his pad in the air, and proclaims, "Allen Williams, you just may have one more left in you!"

He looks around the room, tosses his pad onto the table, and starts picking up beer and other booze bottles. Leaving the room with an armful, he crashes the bottles into the trash bin in the kitchen.

The next morning, the doorbell rings. Al makes his way to the front of a remarkably clean apartment. It is Lorna dropping off the kids for the next couple of days.

As he opens the door, Lorna says, "You know it's Saturday. You got 'em for the next couple of days, Al."

Two kids shout, "Hi, Daddy!" as they race to the TV.

Lorna pokes her nose into the family room. "Wow, you cleaned up the place… or you got maid service. Hah, I know it can't be that."

As she goes to leave, Lorna asks, "By the way, what about the support check?"

He says, "I'm working on it."

Through the closed door, Lorna warns, "Allen, don't make me have to get legal on you."

"I said I'm working on it."

Al turns to the kids and starts teasing and joking with them. Despite the split with Lorna, Al still has a wonderful rapport with Cindy and Jimmy.

After a while, he says, "You kids watch TV for a while so Daddy can do some writing."

As the TV is warming up, the kids begin fighting over the remote. Al settles things by claiming the remote. Much to the chagrin of the kids, he checks the network news channel and sees yet another story about Enceladus.

Jimmy says, "Daddy, can't we watch cartoons?"

"Yeah, just one minute."

TV announcer: "This could be one of the greatest discoveries of our generation. In other news…"

Al says, "OK, here's the remote."

He hands it to the older child, Cindy, who gleefully grabs it.

"Now, you two be fair about what to watch together. I don't want to have to come out of my office to do any conflict resolution."

Al sees the notepad on the coffee table he'd been working on and grabs it.

As he turns to retreat to his office, Cindy says, "Mommy keeps asking, 'When are you going to write something good again?'"

Al stops, pauses, and says, "Cindy, I think I'm really on to something."

"Mommy will be glad to hear that!"

With a knowing grin, Al proceeds to the office and sits down at his cluttered desk. Papers and books litter the surface, along with his pile of unopened letters. He swipes the debris aside to find his laptop buried underneath. He opens up the lid—something he hasn't done in a long while. He sets up his notes and opens a browser. Using Wikipedia, he starts referencing many of his topics, such as Saturn, Enceladus, cryovolcanoes, and Cassini… all the time, jotting further notes, page after page.

The light in the room has visibly receded as Al has been researching for several hours. He yawns and stretches out.

He strikes a thoughtful pose and ponders, "What will be the twist?"

He thinks hard, his eyes darting around the room as if looking for a clue. He sees his cherished copy of H. P. Lovecraft's Mountains of Madness on a shelf. On the other side of the room, he notices a 3D figure depicting the strata of the Grand Canyon. He goes over to examine it, grabs it, and returns to the laptop.

After a long pause, his eyes light up, and he exclaims, "That's it!"

The carbon traces are NOT from the bottom of the trench, but rather…

He begins to search for images of ice trenches, rock strata, Enceladus pictures, etc., on his laptop. With his limited Photoshop skills, he creates an image to materialize his vision. He rests his head on his folded hands, admiring and contemplating his work. His eyes are filled with an enthusiasm he hasn't felt since his early writing days. Suddenly, he hears a yelp from the other room. He has completely forgotten that kids are here.

"Those kids!" he mutters as he gets up to see what the commotion is all about.

"Hey, what's going on in here?"

The kids just giggle and chatter.

"Who's hungry?"

"Yeah! Let's get burgers!"

"Yup, and we're getting the meals… make 'em large sizes, too! We're celebrating!"

Back in the office, on the computer, is a mock-up of the title page for Enceladus. Looking slightly up from within an Enceladus trench with Saturn prominently off in the distance.

On Tuesday, Al drops the kids off back at Lorna's house since their divorce three years before she had gotten remarried.

After the kids are safely in the house and the door closes, Al clasps his hands together. "Alright, time to get 'er going!" as he anticipates doing some major, uninterrupted work on his novel.

He gets home and quickly shuffles to the office, which is now very neat and orderly. Quite obviously, Al has gotten it together. Sipping from a tall mug of coffee, he starts typing away, beginning with Chapter 1, The Carbon Detection. This is pretty much taken from the actual events of the day.

He lights a cigarette, then thinks for a moment and stubs it out. Now is the time to clean up this vice also. He finishes Chapter 1 by bedtime. The next day, he starts Chapter 2, Mission of the Trench Probe. Several days later comes Unexpected Discovery and here's where things start getting interesting. His writing binge continues as he proceeds with Carbon Dating. After several weeks, Sectional Slice Sampling emerges. At last, the final chapter begins to materialize with Micron-Slice Imaging.

Some weeks in, Al appears disheveled but still enthusiastic. He types the final line of the book when the main character says, "I didn't see THAT coming!"

He adds several line spaces and types THE END, finally doing a fist pump. With quiet enthusiasm and pride, he sends his new novel to the publisher. He envisions the reprisal of success, which he once enjoyed.

Within a week, he receives a reply from the publisher. With pride and confidence, he excitedly opens the letter. "REJECTED". Al is stunned. He shakes his head in disbelief. Denial sets in almost immediately. He scrambles to find his phone and calls his agent to get a direct explanation for the rejection.

As he listens, he interjects with an occasional "But…" And finally, "Did they read it?"

The longer he is on the phone, the more he descends into anger and despair. He ends the call without speaking and looks off in the distance, dismayed.

He kicks over a table, then a chair. "I've gotta get OUTTA here!"

As he walks the streets with hands in pockets and head hanging low, he comes across a bar. Pausing in front, he pulls the wadded-up rejection notice out of his pocket and tosses it into the sidewalk trash can. There's nothing left for him to do but grab the door handle and enter the bar.

***

Seven years later, on the deck of the Herschel spacecraft, the surface of Enceladus appears to fill the expansive front viewport. The desolate, bumpy ice surface extends for miles, interrupted only by an occasional ancient impact crater. Two astronauts are in adjacent pilot seats, flipping switches and reading from a multitude of monitors displaying graphics and data of the planet below, as well as the ship's position. One prominently positioned large monitor is a live video feed looking directly downward. The screen is filled with the ice surface, slashed by a deep trench running horizontally. This trench is one of the 'tiger stripes' along the planet's South Pole. When Enceladus's orbit is close to Saturn, these tiger stripe trenches emit the cryovolcanic plumes upon which an early probe detected carbon traces.

However, now that the orbit is further away, the plumes are diminished. The craft is poised to 'drop' the probe into the trench to investigate. With the planet's 33-day orbit, the mission has about a 16-day window in which to deploy the probe.

Commander Ander Slayton issues the command to prepare for probe deployment. First Pilot James Gagarin presses a series of buttons. Shutters begin covering the front bay windows; at the same time, a 360-degree panoramic video screen array lowers on the mid-section of the main deck, surrounding a single chair in the middle. The deck is lit only by the glowing video screens and strategically placed spotlights. Slayton leaves his pilot chair and floats in the zero-G to position himself in the video screen command chair. He pulls up a video monitor attached to the chair. Gagarin remains in the other pilot seat to control the ship's position during probe deployment. Once Clayton is ready, he taps a series of buttons on the monitor and then issues the command to release the probe. The bay doors open with a low-level clunking sound, and the black screens of the 360-display begin to show a splendid, full panoramic view of the Enceladus surface.

For the ship's log, Clayton notes, "The Herschel is now deploying the discovery probe." After the probe has descended about 100 meters, Slayton uses a joystick attached to the command chair to tip the probe 90 degrees so it looks perpendicular to the surface. On the control monitor, a 3D wireframe of the probe simulates the rotation. On one side of the 360-

display is the trench, and on the opposite side is Herschel's belly, with the open bay doors for the probe. The side panels of the 360-display show a view down the stretch of the trench. The ship is getting smaller and smaller as the chasm of the trench looms larger and larger. As the probe descends into the mouth of the ink-black trench, Slayton initiates the halogen lamps on the probe. He is thrilled by the distance he can see down into the trench. The probe is now 50 meters deep into the trench. On one 360-display panel, a line-drawing overlay is illuminated that shows a two-dimensional cross-section of the trench with a small blip indicating the probe. With the joystick, Slayton rotates the probe on its vertical axis so that side panels show the trench walls as the probe continues to descend.

At about halfway to the underground ocean, roughly five kilometers deep into the trench, Clayton looks at the side panels and does a double-take. He notices dark demarcations in the trench walls—on both sides. He rotates the probe so it is facing the trench wall. This demarcation has a height of about 30 meters. It all starts with a single, definitive line. The dark strata are dense and dark at the top and then start to gradually lighten as they descend deeper into the trench.

"Are you seeing this, Jim?" Clayton asks Gagarin.

Looking at his monitor in the pilot's chair, Gagarin can see the frontal view of the probe.

"Yeah… We gotta take a closer look at that."

Clayton reports into the microphone, "We are approximately 4,840 meters deep into the trench and are about to defer the probe descent to examine a peculiar demarcation in the trench walls."

Clayton controls the probe to come within 10 meters of the strata. Unlike the smooth, continuous ice above the top of the strata, the fine layers of dark strata are variable in density and are rough, with some strands protruding from the wall. Upon closer observation, it becomes quite clear that the strata started sporadically and built up more densely as they reached a definitive and abrupt conclusion.

Clayton yells over, "Jim, put the ship in auto-pilot with GPS lock and come look at this."

Clayton reports his strata observations into the mic as Jim presses several monitor buttons to lock the ship's course onto a GPS point on Enceladus. Jim unbuckles his seat belt to come look at the strata in the 360-display. He floats over and slips under the 360-display monitors.

They both peer at the strata with wide eyes and gaping mouths until Jim asks, "Are you thinking what I'm thinking?"

Anders responds, "I'm not sure, but if this is the source of our carbon traces, then we are looking at the slow and steady evolution of a species that developed to a high degree...before it was wiped out by...by some cataclysmic event."

Jim adds, "And judging by how DEEP this is, we're talking about millions of years old. Hard to say more exactly until we do some carbon dating, adjusted for Enceladus, of course."

Jim looks at Anders: "Earth will be getting this feed—and your report—in about an hour and a half. We'd better make sure we're careful with our words, Sir. This is gonna be HUGE."

***

Back on Earth, the TV screen in the store window showed the headline, "ANCIENT LIFE ON ENCELADUS?" It is the same screen on a TV in a pub, in Times Square, in a family's home, and in various languages. The topic began to be the talk of the town…the nation…the world.

All levels of society could relate to the story unfolding. It became common for people of different classes to strike up conversations on the topic with each other. It was the story the world needed to bring the chaotic, opinionated, and varied souls into a sense of community. To think, finally, after all the speculation about extraterrestrial life—here it is, for real. But what is it? Plant? Animal? Some new classification of living creatures?

At the NASA center, a press conference to report the latest findings from the Herschel space mission is about to start. All news networks are there to cover the latest. The people of the world are on the edge of their seats to hear the exciting discoveries unfolding. A presenter stands next to a wall of huge video screens, each displaying windows ready for interaction. The first large screen shows the video feed from the Herschel during the probe descent in the trench. The image is of the strata stripes, from the definitive "starting" line at the bottom, building logarithmically until it comes to an abrupt stop at the top. A second screen shows a graphic illustration of a cross-section of the trench from top to bottom, with a sprite representing the location of the probe.

Reports had just started trickling in about a little-known story written seven years earlier and posted to a science fiction site. This story described a mission such as the Herschel spacecraft had undertaken. The world was abuzz that the author had NAILED it—in so many details. In particular, the carbon traces were NOT from the bottom of the trench, as assumed by the scientists, but from exposed layers within the side walls of the trench. Twitter was ablaze with discussions and speculation.

It didn't take long before the author was identified, and people wanted to find him and talk to him. Since Allen Williams did not come forward and no one knew of his whereabouts, a huge media blitz began in attempts to track down this "prophet of the Enceladus discovery." Now, when the news reported on the unfolding developments, a slate would follow with what looked like a wanted poster for Al. Within a day, news crews were able to track down ex-wife Lorna Sinkowitz. She didn't have many nice things to say about him, mostly confirming that he had a lot of difficulties before his disappearance. His last message to her was that he had had it and was going to check out. She had filed a missing-persons report back then, but he never turned up, so she figured he'd dropped off the radar or maybe even committed suicide.

Back at the Herschel, Clayton and Gagarin are preparing the NASA-provided equipment to do a Magnetic Resonance Imaging (MRI) scan on the block segment extracted from the trench wall from where the "earlier" beginnings of the dark strata appeared, in what is speculated to be the early evolution of life. The MRI can only scan material in a 3' by 3' by 8' slab. With MRI scans, scientists believe that each micro-slice represents many years (units) of time.

In a skid-row park where all the bums and druggies hang out, one particular homeless man rolls over on the bench he has claimed as his territory, at least for this night. His matted hair completely covers his face. It is mid-day, and he is still sleeping it off from the night before. He knows when the sun starts hitting him, it's time to get up for the daily routine of food-finding—dumpster diving. He gets up and staggers around, trying to reclaim his equilibrium. He immediately heads over to the Denny's dumpster, where there is usually an ample amount of food thrown away. It's his lucky day, as someone has discarded a to-go box containing practically a whole meal. As he clears his unkempt bangs from his face to eat, we see it is Al. Matted hair and beard, both graying, probably not washed for months.

On his way back to the park, Al passes a pawn shop. Glancing in the window at the numerous items for sale, he notices a flat-screen TV on which a reporter is interviewing Lorna. Al does an immediate double-take, not believing what he has seen. He rubs his eyes and squints hard to get a better look. He puts his ear up to the window to hear the audio, but that's useless, as the TV is muted. When he looks back at the screen, it shows the slate of him with the title, "The Search Continues for Allen Williams."

Al yells, "Hey! Heyyyy, that's me!" as he instinctively starts pounding on the plate-glass window.

The pawn shop owner comes out with a broom. "HEY! You bum! Get away from the window!"

As Al steps away from poking with the broom, he accidentally backs into a couple of thugs with loads of chips on their shoulders.

"Humph!" One of the thugs shouts, "Hey, dickhead!"

They both shove Al with full might as one shout, "Watch where you're going, fuckin' bum!"

Having slight body weight, Al goes stumbling for several steps before flying head-first into the cement base of a chain-linked fence down a narrow alley. His frail frame just slumps in place, motionless, facedown, and bent backward. The thugs don't even notice as they continue their menacing walk. Several people walk by and glance at Al, thinking he's just that a drunk sleepin' it off. Eventually, a concerned passerby phones 911 when she notices the blood seeping down the sidewalk.

At the next NASA briefing, scientists are displaying the micro-slice image frames taken by the MRI on the Herschel. Tiny shapes are highlighted and described as having once been living organisms. Due to the relatively small sampling that can be taken, many organisms are cut off at the edges of the block sample. This is only the beginning. Scientists are giddy with anticipation, knowing that the strata near the top are highly condensed and more recent chronologically. How developed were these species, and how did they meet their demise?

In a hospital ICU, there is an indigent care patient clinging to life, with bandages covering half his face and multiple tubes in his arms, face, and other places not seen. At the nursing station just outside his room, a small group of doctors and nurses banter during a lull period. Al begins to slowly wake up and looks around sleepily, trying to figure out where he is. He is very groggy, and his eyes have trouble focusing.

There is a muted TV in his room showing CNN. It seems they're covering some conflict in the Middle East. After a commercial, there's a teaser of upcoming news segments, one of which is the story of the continued search for Allen Williams. Sure enough, his image pops up on the screen. Al's eyes flutter wide, and the ECG and EKG machines begin to accelerate. The auto-morphine drip line kicks in due to Al's heightened vital signs. His eyes become heavy and difficult to open.

Tamika comes in to check on him, but he's back in his vegetative state. She begins to leave the room but notices the news of Al on the TV. She pauses, makes a contorted funny face, and then whips out her smartphone to look up a news site. Expanding a photo to fill her screen, she holds it up next to Al's face. She hurriedly comes out to the nursing station to find a couple of co-workers.

"Hey, you know, I think the John Doe we just got might be that Allen Williams they're looking for."

The others, doubting, "Yeah, sure."

During her break, Tamika goes to Al's room to give him a good grooming, starting with a shave. She gets him cleaned up, steps back, and proudly exclaims, "Yes, sirree, this IS our guy".

Later that evening, a small group of doctors and nurses gathered to see Tamika's claim. Al slowly opens his eyes halfway. He notices the group in front of him and laboredly says, "Have they done the micro-slice imaging yet?" Most of the group laugh and cry at the same time.

One doctor proudly says, "Yup, he's our man!"

***

Twelve years later, the specially designed space lab for the Enceladus Genesis Project (EGP) hosts the most sophisticated MRI device imaginable, capable of scanning a 20-foot cube, and built just for the EGP mission. Three research scientists are completing a full scan of Block #2, extracted from the trench wall. They had already determined from Block #1, taken from the initial dark stripe, that the planet had been hit by an asteroid carrying large amounts of carbon. As the huge rotational arm of the MRI slows down, three people flock to the display monitor. Upon closer inspection, we see their names are Dr. Hugo Bohm, Dr. Samantha Ziegler, and Dr. Allen Williams – given an honorary doctorate for his contribution. Dr. Bohm operates the touch screen and begins parsing the three-dimensional image, rotating the block upon various axes and fixing it on the transverse plane. They start at the bottom, or the oldest, and move sequentially upward chronologically through time. Sam and Al quickly begin pointing out some of the already chronicled species of flora and fauna. In their haste to examine what new species may await them in this scan, none of the three notice a red warning light off to the side.

From his pilot's seat, Commander Bishop sees a warning indicator coming from the lab. He selects the blinking red button. It states: MRI Power ON.

On the intercom, he says, "Dr. Williams, did you forget to turn off the MRI power after that last scan?"

Al looks over at the control panel and says, "Oh shit! Yeah…sorry."

As he reaches over to flip the switch back off, something catches his eye in the reflection of a shiny plate—something is moving behind them. He slowly looks behind the three of them toward the block. His eyes bulge. "Kids, we've got a new chapter to my book."

The other two scientists turn toward Al, and then follow his gaze to look behind them. Their eyes bulge, and their jaws slowly drop.

The three of them stare like deers caught in the headlights as a greenish-blue ghost-like figure, slightly undulating, begins rising out of Block # 2.

Al quips "Wow. Now, I didn't see THAT coming."

END

ERROR 404 - Page Not Found

Bruce Clark Bennett ©2020

Pitch-black, the sound of a person slightly snoring. The snoring becomes irregular, then interspersed with moaning… not just any moan, but the kind when someone is having a nightmare. After a loud yelp, a man wakes up thrashing and in a pool of sweat. After catching his breath, he chuckles, realizing it was just a dream. It's that CLOCK-thing again. He already knows what time it is but looks at his bedside alarm clock radio anyway. Grabs it with his hand and turns it to see the time, dimly illuminating his squinting, scrunched-up face. He lifts it slightly and slams it back onto the nightstand. "Knew it!" He slams his head back into his pillow and screams, "Argh!!" He knows he's not going to fall back to sleep anytime soon, so he fumbles around for his bedside tablet. He turns it on, and the dim light of the screen illuminates his face to see his tired, angry face. After a short while of skipping from website to website, he notices something. His eyes grow large in unison with a look of disgust. "Noooo!.... NOOOOOOO!" After smacking his tablet a couple of times, he yells, "SHIT!" and throws his tablet across the room, wiping out several glasses and fragile things on his dresser bureau. In the dark, he yells, "God DAMN IT!!". Then, only the sound of heavy breathing. And the pitch-black.

A MONTH EARLIER

It is morning, and James is getting up and preparing for work at his modern, tech-savvy apartment. In the bathroom shaving; in the kitchen eating. He walks past the muted TV while on his phone, talking to a colleague. The TV has the news about a local proposition – one that is widely controversial and prompting confrontational debate – Prop 404. Before long, he gets his travel mug with a homemade espresso drink, turns off the TV, grabs his bag, heads to the door, and is on his way to his job. He has been the manager of the IT department at MarComOne for four months now. He loves his job, and the money is good… very good. He had been programming at the company for about 4 years before the promotion. He made an impression with his web designs and coding, and his bosses took notice.

Living at the Infinity condos at Folsom and Spear Streets in San Francisco, James has an idyllic walk to work. Only 4 city blocks away from his office on Market Street. As he strolls to work, there are several displays of 404 that go unnoticed in the background. Billboard advert; building address 404 6th Street; a homeless-looking guy carrying a sign: PSALMS 40:4; Lawyer who primarily defends DUIs with telephone # 415-404-0404. At one point in his walk, he has to maneuver around a homeless encampment – the low point of his daily journey.

He enters the building where MarComOne is located, a company that provides web-based marketing services for high-class clientele. MarComOne has half the 18th floor in the tower at 330 Market St., San Francisco. Now, with about 40 employees, they are growing rapidly. Rumor has it that they may be getting another fourth of the 18th floor soon. IT and programming had been under the auspices of the Operations Manager, but as the company has been expanding, the need for middle managers has arisen. As IT Manager, James oversees two programmers and one junior IT guy.

After several "good mornings" on the way to his office, James arrives at his desk, plops down his shoulder bag, and fires up his computer while holding his homemade double latte in hand. He is at the computer, on the phone, looking out the window, and arranging the photos on his shelves. On the wall are several certificates of recognition from the company, which he slightly tilts to get perfect alignment. While on the computer checking email, he gets a call from one of the programmers. Naveen has called in sick today - it must be that flu going around. They were supposed to go live with a new webpage to their site in a couple of days, but with Naveen out, James would have to pick it up, code it, test it, and send it to Quality Control before final posting. He opens the programming tools on his computer and gets to work.

After coding for an hour or so, he starts testing the webpage he has set up. All elements appear properly on his screen, with graphics displaying and in alignment. He starts testing the hyperlinks established on the screen. He gets to the last link that is supposed to link to the FAQ page, but when he clicks it, he gets the browser program error: 404 – Page Not Found. Annoyed, he frowns and shakes his head. He must have made a typo. He double-checks the webpage URLs to confirm. The URLs are long, so he takes a moment to go character by character to compare. Hmmm, they seem correct. Maybe he didn't save the last version of the screen code. He does so and re-tests the link. Again, Error 404. Shaking his head, he opens another browser window and types letter-by-letter, the URL for the hyperlink. The page comes up as it should. He selects the URL from the browser and pastes it into the code. Saves it, opens updated HTML, then tests the link… Error 404. After a frustrating sigh and frown, he picks up the phone to call the newest programmer, Malik, to take a look at the code. Malik was hired to fill James' position upon his promotion. "Hey, Malik, James here. I'm gonna send you a link to a new webpage – test it out for me when you get a chance, would ya?" He gets a "Sure, boss. 15 minutes from now? I've got to get this email to Jenny in HR." James says, "Yeah, no problem (pause); look for the email," and proceeds to copy the URL to an email and shoots it over to Malik. James proceeds on to another task on his to-do list.

After 30 minutes, James calls Malik, "Malik, were you able to take a look at that?" Malik responds, "I'm just finishing it up now, boss." James: "You tested the FAQ link yet?" Malik: "Doing it just as we speak. (pause) Yeah, looks fine." James, with a surprised look, "Hey, hold on," as he re-opens the window with a programmed new page on it. He clicks the FAQ link, and sure enough, it works fine. "Malik, did you do anything with the code?" Malik: "No, why?" James: "Huh… Oh, nothing. Thanks for checking that out for me." Malik, with a slight eyebrow raised, "Yeah, no problem." He hangs up the phone and shakes off a 'whatever' expression.

At the end of the day, James is walking home from the office. He can't stop thinking about the 404 Error he struggled with that mysteriously disappeared – and what eats at him is why he couldn't figure it out. There are a couple more unnoticed 404s in the background. He glances up to see the green WALK-light and looks down at the curb to step into the street. Suddenly, an older businessman grabs him by the shoulder and yanks him back onto the sidewalk as a bus whooshes by, much too close for comfort. James sees the back of the bus speeding away and squints to see the route-number identifier on the bus – it is the 404 bus. The businessman says to James, "Kid, you better pay more attention to where you're going. You almost got killed!" James collects himself and says, "Thanks. I got a lot on my mind lately." He doesn't dare mention he thought he saw a green WALK signal.

A shaken James arrives at his condo-lofts building and checks his mailbox. Good, no bills today. He steps into the waiting elevator and presses floor 6. The car stops on floor 4, and the door opens, but nobody is there. A room door across and to the left from the elevator just closes, and James just happens to notice it is pad number 404. He'd been living in the building for more than 4 years - 4 years, 04 months, to be exact - and he had never noticed that before. Then again, aside from the programming error, the number 404 never really meant anything to him until today. He pops his head out of the elevator to see if anyone is around. He shrugs it off and presses the button to close the elevator doors to continue to his floor. Just then, the 404 door opens to just a slit and slams shut by the time the elevator doors close. Back at his condo, he gets comfortable - sheds his suit, lights a small roach from a stash, and sits down with a beer - in front of the picture window overlooking the Bay. He just sits pondering the incidents of the day.

A couple of days pass with no incidence with the number 404. He's convinced it was just a weird coincidence and relieved it seems to be over. However, he does find himself noticing occurrences of the number 404 – in addresses, adverts, etc.

Wednesday, while going to work, James gets on the elevator going down, and several people are already in the car. He glances to see if anyone makes eye contact, but they're glued to their phones. It stops on floor 4, but there is no one there to get on. On Monday, he noticed the room door for 404 slammed shut. He thinks nothing of it, but just as the elevator doors are closing, the door to room 404 opens just enough to see a ghostly face. As James tries to focus harder, the elevator doors shut, and he coyly looks at the other two people in the elevator, but neither of them notices as they are engrossed in their cellphones – just a couple more "smombies." While in the lobby, James goes over to the mailboxes to see the name listed for room 404; it appears to be scratched out. He looks around, then pulls out his phone camera and takes a quick photo.

James is haunted by the visual of the ghost-like face all day. On his travels back home, walking through the homeless encampment, he briefly sees the same ghostly face on some stranger. As he is taken aback by the vision, the stranger takes notice and is offended by James' obvious focus of disgust. The man says, "What the fuck's with you? You got a problem?" James shakes it off and quickly continues on his way, doing his best to avoid confrontation. As soon as he gets home, he downs a shot of vodka.

Later that evening, James is on the computer at his home office, the desk cluttered with several beer bottles. He tries researching the numerology for 4-0-4 and only comes up with the term "tetraphobia," which is the fear of the number four. There seems to be nothing specific about 404, no such thing as "404-phobia"- at least that has been documented. After a while, he leans back and says to himself, "Looks like I'm venturing into uncharted territory." After he leaves for the bathroom, the email notifications pop up on his computer screen – three messages, with one from a sender 404. The notifications slowly fade from the screen. Later, when he returns to his computer, he sees the email from 404. He opens it, but it's blank. When he tries replying to the email, he gets an email sending error – the server does not exist.

Thursday at work, he gets a message that a departmental meeting has been scheduled at 4 o'clock with the CEO and other department heads. He stresses over deciding whether to go on time or arrive AFTER 4:04 to make sure nothing goes wrong during the meeting. He decides he had better attend on time since the hard-driving CEO will be there and James has to give a status report for his department. At 4 o'clock, people assemble and get prepared for the first few minutes, but James, with heart pounding, can't help but focus on the digital clock as it approaches 4:04. As the clock hits 4:04, he is transfixed on the clock and all the voices and sounds dim down. After a few moments, all of a sudden, Sally, the operations manager, clearly perturbed, loudly says, "James!" He quickly looks at her and notices everyone at the table is staring at him. Even the CEO slowly raises his eyes from his tablet to look up at James. He glances back at the clock, but now it is 4:09. Sally says, "Are you alright??" Then, clearly annoyed, "Do you have something better to do at this time?" He sheepishly apologizes for spacing out, collects himself, and proceeds to give his report, stumbling through. After giving his report, he has a huge feeling of relief, but all he can do is think to himself, "What the hell! Where did the five minutes go??" After the meeting, Sally tells James she wants to see him in her office. Once in her office, she tells him that she is concerned about his behavior and asks if he needs some time off. He declines the time off and assures her that he will clear the distraction that has been annoying him the past few days – of course, not telling her of the details.

The experience eats at him the rest of the day, night, and most of the next day. He watches the clock go from 4:04 to 4:05 without incident. He begins to notice the number more and more in his surroundings but with no occurring incidence.

10 minutes – Paradise Lost

It's Friday, and James is so relieved that it is the end of the week - a tough one at that. He lays in bed, ready for sleep – he wants to be ready for later. His girlfriend, Heather, plans on coming over for the night after she gets off from her nursing job. Sometimes, it is early morning when her shift ends, depending on the activity in the ER. James is accustomed to her late nights and looks forward to her waking him up when she comes over so they can roll around in the sheets. He awakes upon hearing her drop her bag on the floor, and she starts undressing. She says to him, "Hey you." He glances over at the alarm clock on the nightstand and sees the time – 4:04 a.m. He does a quick double-take and just says to himself, "Oh no." She slaps his naked ass to get his attention; he rolls & turns to see her undoing her bra and tossing it aside. As she starts to crawl into bed, he quickly turns to see the clock. Close-up of his eyes as they bulge out… it is 4:15 a.m. He notices his body is covered in sweat. "What the fuck?" he mutters, as he realizes he just missed 10 minutes of sex. She goes, "What? What did you say?" His averting eyes dart around, searching for an answer. He sheepishly asks, "How was it for you?" She bursts out laughing and says, "Ha, Pretty good… Coulda been a little longer," with a wry smile. She snuggles up with him and soon falls asleep, but he lays wide awake thinking to himself, "I missed the sex? This must be some kinda hell… or some Twilight Zone episode!"

Once again, several days pass with no incidents, but that does little to quell his feelings of anxiety and apprehension – not knowing when the next incident will occur.

2-Hour Loss

Another company meeting is scheduled for 4 p.m. next Wednesday. He feigns food poisoning and excuses himself to leave early, but not before submitting the IT Department weekly status report to Sally.

He calls for a ride-share and arrives at his condo just before 4 p.m. When taking the elevator up alone to his floor, again it stops on the 4th floor, but nobody is there. His eyes dart to room 404, across from the elevator. Just as the elevator door closes, he reaches his arm through to re-open the doors.

He decides to defy the 404 curse.

As he steps out of the elevator, he looks at his watch and sees it's just a couple of minutes before 4:04. He waits a few minutes, thinking to himself, "What the hell am I doing… am I nuts? " At 4:04, he says, "Fuck it" as he knocks on door 404. There is no answer, then again, so he tries the doorknob – it opens. He first looks both ways down the hallway before proceeding. He ever so slowly opens the door, cautiously looks around, and sneakily enters the room. He peers back out and down the hallway to see if anyone is around. What if it's a trap? The room is dark from the blinds drawn. Just as he enters several steps into the room, the door slams closed behind him. He looks back at the door just as a shriek is heard in front of him. He hears a crescendo chant, "four-oh-four-oh-FOUR-OH-" He turns to see a horrifying face flying his way. He screams. Blackness.

He "wakes up" standing in front of his own door #664 – quickly bracing himself on the door sill. He is unaware of the events of what took place - of what, and for how long? He panics as he looks at his watch - it is a quarter past six – two hours! WTF! His eyes pop. He tries to relax, taking long breaths, but he is trembling as he fumbles for his keys and enters his pad. The door swings open, he falls through the door and lands on all fours. He kicks the door closed and crawls to the nearby couch. He plops down face up, covers his face with both hands, and lets out an "Aargh!" After several deep breaths, he finally calms down. He contemplates for a while; then, he moves his hands down off his face to reveal a black eye. He starts touching it and feels the pain. He springs up and looks in the mirror to see the new shiner. He looks away and says, "I don't fucking believe this!" He defiantly heads for the door to pay a visit to room 404. He presses the elevator button, but it takes too long for his limited patience, so he races down the two floors via the stairs. Once at the door, he forcefully tries the knob. The door is locked now, so he pounds on the door. He looks around to see if anyone is around and then kicks at the door. Someone pops their head out of a nearby room and says, "Keep it up… and I'm calling the cops!" Just before he leaves, he peeks in the peephole for movement. A strong red laser light stings his eyes, and he stumbles backward and staggers back to his condo. The neighbor who threatened with the cop-call mutters, "Asshole."

He gets back to his apartment and finds his bag leaning against his door. He momentarily freezes in shock as he has completely forgotten about his bag. He quickly checks if anything is missing, but it appears to be there.

After entering his pad, he looks in the mirror and examines his face. He tends to his bruises with a frozen bag of peas. He rubs his eye, which still has a massive retinal burn. Anxiety creeps in as he dwells on the prospect that he may have sustained permanent damage.

The following few days at work, he is kidded by his colleagues and subordinates about his shiner. As he leaves the breakroom, one snickering fellow says to the other, "You do NOT talk about Fight Club," as the other laughs. James sheepishly returns to his office, avoiding further social interaction.

A week goes by without an incident – no 404 scares or losses of experience. Despite vigilance, he notices no occurrences with room 404. He begins to convince himself that it is a passing thing.

Half Day Be Gone

It is early morning Saturday, and James is sound asleep. On the nightstand, there are 4 beer bottles and a half-spent joint in the ashtray. He awakens from a dream where he sees the haunting face at 3:55. After collecting himself, he looks around to see if Heather has stopped by, but she has not. He rests his head on the pillow, staring at the clock, wanting to see what happens when it hits 4:04. As the minutes slowly go by, his eyelids are just too heavy to keep open.

All of a sudden, he is jolted awake as he hears a loud voice. He flutters his eyelids, trying to wake up; he rolls over to glance at the clock - 4:05. He sits up and starts rubbing his eyes. Heather grabs him and starts shaking him, "What the hell are you doing!?" Still trying to awaken, he grunts, "What? What's wrong?" She says: "Sleeping all day?! It's four in the afternoon now!" He quickly looks again at the clock and notices the PM indicator as she opens the drapes to let the sun in. She exits towards the bathroom, spouting complaints about getting a double shift last night and how understaffed they are at the hospital. But he doesn't hear her. He just lays there in shock at the notion that he has just lost 12 hours. He feels his stomach twisting and knotting up, along with an emptiness inside he has never experienced.

He refrains from telling her the truth and instead explains that he hasn't been sleeping well the last few days and that he slept in to make up for lost sleep. Along with her lack of sleep and crankiness, they both decide that they are not the best company for each other today, so Heather leaves to crash at her apartment with the excuse that she needs to make up for her lack of sleep. After she leaves, James cannot dismiss the angst he feels and vows to turn a new leaf. He starts by dumping all his weed & booze. That evening, James calls Heather to meet for dinner. He decides to tell her everything… "Listen, babe, I've got to tell you something…" However, she is not completely understanding. "Really, James? A number? A number is making you mess up? How can you blame a number for your fuck-ups? (Pause) I think you need some space to work this thing out, James," as the call abruptly ends.

James has a dream that night. In front of him are two hands holding up a large book with the title "James Randle Dougherty," the face of the holder is obscured by the book. With the book facing him, the hands open the book to chapter 28 (James' age), but some of the sentences begin disappearing before his eyes; the book lowers, revealing Sally's face. The book raises again, but the hands are different, more masculine. The hands flip the pages to chapter 29, but it is blank. The book lowers to reveal God. Again, the book rises, and this time, the hands are dark & grotesque. The hands flip through the entire book from the beginning – and it is blank. A hideous, mocking laugh begins as the book lowers to reveal a Devil-like figure. James gasps and is awoken by a phone call – it is Sally, wondering where he is. His heart pounding, he sheepishly tells Sally his alarm didn't go off.

A few days later, he reconciles with Heather, and the two go on a date. After watching a movie, they stop at a café where she suggests he take a vacation. Perhaps it will help him shake this 404 obsession he's going through. He ponders the notion and agrees that it might be a good solution.

While James is back home, he begins to look for his passport in his file folder of important documents. He finds his birth certificate. As he pauses over it, he realizes he was born at 4:04 PM on April 4th, 1990… 4:04. This is cause for much contemplation.

In the meantime, things stabilize at work as he has no experience with missing time. Relationships normalize, and things seem to be back on track.

His Birthday is coming up on April 4th, and his apprehension becomes crippling - knowing that SOMETHING is going to happen that day. Fortunately, his company allows employees to take the day off on their Birthdays – which is a godsend to him, knowing for certain that something is bound to happen on that day. Heather suggests partying out on the town on his B-day to forget his problem, but he persuades her that he just wants to hang out at his place with her.

What a Day – That Wasn't

On the evening of April 3rd, James tells Heather he really needs her and to please, PLEASE come home right after ER duty. She assures him, "Yeah, sure, baby."

It is April 4th at 4 in the morning… she calls him from the ER, but his phone is on vibrate, and he doesn't wake up to answer. The phone vibrates off the table and onto a pile of clothing strewn on the hardwood floor in a muffled sound. She leaves a message, "There was a bad bus crash an hour ago… Sorry baby, it's all hands on deck for double shifts. I'll call you when I get free… I promise." Behind her on an ICU TV is the newscast of the bus crash, Trans-Rout schedule 404. Back at James' place, a close-up of his phone sees the time at 4:04, then times out and fades away. The ER is overrun with trauma admissions; Heather crashes there at the hospital with several other nurses and a couple of doctors. She makes eye contact with the good-looking new intern. They both coyly smile.

James has a dream about seeing a psychiatrist - Freud-like, with a German accent. "Yes, you have '404-Phoboia…'"

James: "There's an official name for it? I KNEW IT! And… and so, are there others that have it, really?"

Psych turns into a lunatic: "No, NOT really!… You're just NUTS! A WACKO!" as the Psycho-psych shoves a 404 sign in James' face. After a loud yelp, he wakes up thrashing and in a pool of sweat. After catching his breath, he chuckles, realizing it was just a dream. It's that CLOCK-thing again. He already knows what time it is but looks at his bedside alarm clock radio anyway. Grabs it with his hand and turns it to see the time, dimly illuminating his squinting, scrunched-up face. He lifts it slightly and slams it back onto the nightstand. "Knew it!" He smashes his head back into his pillow and screams, "Argh!!" He knows he's not going to fall back to sleep anytime soon, so he fumbles around for his bedside tablet. He turns it on, and the dim light of the screen illuminates his face to see his tired, angry face. After a short while of skipping from website to website, he notices something. His eyes grow large in unison with a look of disgust. "Noooo!.... NOOOOOOO!" After smacking his tablet a couple of times, he yells, "SHIT!" and throws his tablet across the room, wiping out several glasses & fragile things on his dresser bureau. In the dark, he yells, "God DAMN IT!!" Then, only the sound of heavy breathing. And the pitch-black.

He screams, "I LOST 24 FUCKING HOURS… THIS HAS GOT TO STOP!" He looks around, "Where's my phone?" He turns the light on and knocks over several items on his nightstand. He looks on the floor and discovers his phone in a pile of clothes. He finds a dozen messages on it from Heather. He listens to several and then calls her but gets her voicemail. He says, "Sorry babe, my phone was on vibrate the past 24 hours… which I lost. I need help." Back at the hospital, Heather's silent phone displays the message received, while on the other side of the room, Heather and the intern are embraced in a long kiss.

On Monday, James meets with Sally and tries to explain his situation - without venturing to admit he's having a nervous breakdown… over a number of things. She agrees to give him some time off and admits that she would not do this for just any employee on such short notice. He has over 90 hours of PTO, so she suggests that he take a couple of weeks off to collect himself. After they strike an accord with the time off, she requests a comprehensive status report indicating the current projects being worked on by Malik and Naveen. He says, "Sure, I'll have that on your desk by the end of the day."

Sally says, "If you want to talk to a professional, this guy is one of the best," as she scribbles down a number on a post-it. As she hands him the note, "James, I want you back a hundred percent, okay?" He nods in agreement.

Afterward, Sally is alone in her office typing into a job website (RiteFit.com), posting a position for an IT manager/supervisor.

A Real Psychologist

James is sitting and talking to Dr. Kalesco - as referred by Sally.

Kalesco: "So tell me what's going on with you, James. "

James: "Well, doc, I've got this thing going on with the number four, zero, four. I'll see the number 4-0-4, and something bad will happen... but not all the time; it seems random. Often, it has to do with the time, 4:04. It started small... I'd lose minutes. Then it turned to hours... a half-day. Then, most recently, Saturday, to be precise, a whole day!"

Kalesco: "What do you mean by losing time?"

James: "It's just a blank... I have absolutely no recognition or memory of the blanked-out time." H= changes his composure. "I just don't know when it's gonna happen… it's so random. (Contemplates) It has turned me into a nervous wreck. Knowing it has something to do with the number 404, but not knowing when the anomaly will happen."

Kalesco: "So what is the significance of this number to you, James?"

James: "Never really meant anything to me until a month ago when I got this annoying 404 Error while I was programming a web page with a hyperlink, but when I tested it over and over and over again, it wouldn't work right. I kept getting the Error 404, page not found. That seemed to be the start of it."

James continues to tell Dr. Kalesco of his other experiences with 404, including that he was born at 4:04 on April 4th. And also the room 404 incident.

Kalesco: "So tell me about your mother."

James describes the circumstances of his birth… "I know my mother died after getting broadsided by a drunk driver. She passed away just as I was born."

The sounds and noises of a busy ER. Looking down on a woman being quickly wheeled into the ER operating room. The doctor asks, "What happened?" AMR: "Car accident… Massive internal trauma and bleeding… She's pregnant, 8 or 9 months, I guess."

They saved the baby, but the mother died.

Kalesco: "Do you feel guilty for your mother's death?"

James: "People have told me all my life, "It was not my fault. I feel bad when I think of it… and even have some remorse… but no guilt. (Pause) Should I?"

Kalesco: "Certainly not, as you should not. And what about your father?"

James: "I don't know much about him. He put me up for adoption after my mother's death. I suppose he thought he couldn't raise me on his own. I never tried to find out if he's still alive or not."

Kalesco: "I have some tools and techniques you can try to help you defeat this misperception and delusion."

After several days, James has a reprieve from his 404 phobia. He utilizes the techniques from Dr. Kalesco to deny the existence of the coincidence, minimize, and even negate the validity of the association.

It works well for him, and his confidence flourishes once again. He gets back to his work – and assures Sally he has a new lease on life. He gets back with Heather.

He learns to avoid looking out the elevator when it stops at floor 4 by standing at the side of the elevator to avoid seeing the room number.

He gets to his place and looks over to the adjacent room, #666. "He chuckles and mutters to himself, "Nah, one number curse is ENOUGH."

In Heather's apartment, James explains to her that learning & talking about his biological mother helps him work through this problem. He tells her, "I'm going to the library to hunt down old newspaper archives."

The Library

At the library, James is working at a table with several self-help books about defeating phobias. He uses the microfiche archives to research articles in the SF Examiner newspaper of April 5th, 1990, to locate the news story of his mother's death. He finds it. The DUI driver was Donna O. Deren. He writes the name down and her initials D-O-D; plays with the numerology… D=4… 4 "O" 4. He gets contemplative. At first, he laughs off the discovery. Why does that name seem familiar? Then, with a frown, he gets his phone out and looks at the photo he took of room 404's mailbox. He does max-zoom-in and can barely make out the name Deren despite the scratches.

He begins to Google the name Donna O. Deren - it turns out she has a Wikipedia page. She had been a writer of metaphysical & numerology books up until 1990, when she was convicted of DUI manslaughter for being drunk, running a red light, and smashing the car driven by a pregnant woman. She disappeared soon after her jail time. James discovers an obscure interview she had at a metaphysical bookstore, where she explains the debilitating remorse she felt afterward that stifled her desire to write anymore. He scrolls down the page to investigate the titles she has written. When he clicks the link for her last title about Haunting Numerology, he gets a 404 Error when going to a details page for the specific book. He laughs it off and clicks the Return to Previous Page button on the 404 screen. It loops back to the same 404 Error screen. Again, he laughs it off, but it is less funny this time, and he starts to get aggravated. A third time, he gets another 404 ERROR, but with the words "DON'T YOU GET IT JAMES?" on the screen. He's horrified, and when he beckons the person next to him to see it, the message is gone on the 404 page. The neighbor looks at him weirdly and then cautiously gets up and moves away as James' stare is transfixed on the screen.

He starts getting 404s on every hyperlink. He starts yelling in the library, "It's a figment of my imagination!"…

Louder and louder with every 404 instances.

Absolute paranoia infiltrates his mind. He has a psychotic break while everyone in the library is watching him.

He gets a call from caller ID "404 2U."… He throws his phone at the wall, his eyes darting wildly. Several people are staring in shock but quickly look away to avoid eye contact. He briefly comes to his senses and goes to retrieve his cracked phone from the floor. By this time, everyone is either staring, getting up to clear the area, or plucking their phones out to record the meltdown. He looks around, sees everyone watching, and he goes berserk.

He gets up like a wild animal and runs into an easel, propping up a poster sign for Prop 404, which he starts punching wildly. A young boy watching quips, "Jeez, I guess he really must not like Prop 404". His entranced friend next to him is too enthralled to laugh.

He stumbles toward the main doors when he sees the clock reads 3:45… "I can make it home before THE TIME!" Everyone around is in shock and fear, not knowing what this madman will do next. Some of the young adults are even laughing, thinking it is a prank. Many are already holding their phones up, recording the meltdown, and posting to Twitter, Snapchat, or TikTok.

He runs outside, and a rally for signatures is assembled for Prop 404. He runs and screams, "I gotta get home!!" He stumbles and falls, running to his car. Several protesters begin walking towards him to see if he's all right, but all James sees are the 404s on the placards bearing down on him. He yells, "Get outta my way!" as he gets up and smashes through the group as if it were a gauntlet.

James gets into his car and drives wildly erratic, barely missing other cars… A couple of cars collide, avoiding James' reckless driving. He gets on the freeway and starts speeding, trying to get home before 4:04. His phone rings, and he distractingly fumbles for it, hoping it is Heather. Instead, it is from "404 2U" again. When he looks up from the phone and sees he is about to smash into a slow-moving car just ahead, he veers to the right, off the road, and onto the shoulder. He crashes into the sign-pole – for Exit 404.

From above, he wheeled quickly into an ER, down to the triage area for immediate surgery. The rushing gurney passes by an exhausted nurse ending her shift – Heather, who is just off duty and oblivious to the new patient being wheeled in. She stops and annoying remembers, "Oh shit! James!" as she pulls out her phone to start dialing him. She continues walking to the parking garage.

Back to a top view of James on the gurney, his vitals begin to flat-line. CROSSFADE to his MOTHER 28 years ago on the gurney being wheeled into surgery (same FLASHBACK of earlier when with psychotherapist).

Moments later, doctors attempt to deliver the injured woman's baby. A stillborn baby is born to a surviving mother.

THE END

NeoGenus

By Bruce Clark Bennett – ©2020

There is a human figure fully illuminated in black space. He is struggling for freedom, but there are no restraints on him. His head begins thrashing side to side but then abruptly becomes straightened stiff, looking forward. Suddenly, lightning or electricity is seen converging at his head from various directions. The man screams from the excruciating pain. The field of view grows whiter and whiter until a large BANG is heard.

Jorge wakes up sweating with a yelp, startling his wife sleeping next to him. She comforts him and asks (in Spanish), "That same nightmare, hon?"

"Yeah, it's that one where I'm getting shocked by someone or something… it's the alien abduction!" explains Jorge.

Alice suggests, "Hush up about the aliens! I really think you need to talk to someone about these dreams."

He says, "Aw, they're not that often; besides, how can we afford therapy?" He looks at the clock radio and says, "It's almost 6; I might as well get up. You get more sleep, babe", as he wipes the sleep from his face and puts on some jeans and a tee shirt. In the kitchen, he gets the coffee maker brewing. As the coffee begins dripping into the pot, he gets his smartphone out to read the morning news. As he scans the tabloid news articles for interesting ones, he mutters his contempt for the recent political news. "Gawd, I can't wait till this ELECTION is over! Sick of this. How can so many people get DUPED by this clown!" After the usual heinous crime stories, he clicks over to the science page - he always wished he could have become a scientist, such a fascinating and noble vocation. He reads the headline, TOURISTS IN COSTA RICA MAKE ASTONISHING DISCOVER.

He begins reading the story of how four tourists in the remote jungles of Costa Rica stumbled upon a video camera partially submerged in the soil, believed to have been there for a decade or so. After bringing the camera back to the States with them, one of the techno-nerds was able to retrieve the memory chip from the non-working camera containing the videos and view them. While reading the story, Jorge is interrupted when his stepson enters the kitchen. After starting amicability, several terse comments are traded back and forth. Eventually, young Carlos yells, "You're NOT my dad!" and storms out of the house for school.

Alice sleepily enters the kitchen after being awoken by the loud voices. After several assuring remarks to one another, Alice dictates, "Whatever you do, don't ever tell him that story you told me about being abducted by aliens! Do you think he lacks respect now? If you ever told him that story, he'd never speak to you again." After making them both a quick breakfast, Alice says, "I've got to get ready to go to the hospital." Alice's nursing job is the family's only means of steady income, and Thank God, health insurance for the three of them.

Jorge gives her a kiss and heads out the door, and down the street to the local tree and shrub nursery for any impromptu work he can get. He is met there by other day laborers also looking to get lucky with random jobs. They are all buddies and occasionally will go for a brew at day's end – but only if it has been a productive and profitable day.

The next day, Jorge was lucky to get several jobs during the day along with his buddy Luis. It is a job clearing some wild bushes and shrubs from a long-neglected house on the west side of town. As he and Luis are clearing the bushes next to the house, Luis is startled and taken aback by a large insect that was disturbed by the destruction of its domicile. While Luis is scared and backing away, Jorge approaches and calmly picks up the 6-inch bug. He examines it and tells Luis of its scientific name, "Titanus giganteus. Odd, they're not native to around here." Luis, not caring to hear *anything* about it, shouts in Spanish, "GET RID OF THE DAMN THING!" Jorge, seemingly knowing how to handle the bug without getting pinched or stung, carries it to a nearby field and lets it go unharmed. As he watches it crawl away, he is bemused by the fact that he *know*s the name of the insect. This has happened several other times while out on landscaping jobs. He had dismissed the incidents by rationalizing that before his alien abduction and the subsequent amnesia, he studied insects.

The jobs for today were decent paying, AND it was Friday, so five of the guys headed for the pub for a couple of cold brews. While sitting at the bar, the TV behind Jorge has the news on. There is a story of the ongoing saga of the tourists who found the mysterious video camera. The audio was off, so it was only the video displaying with closed captions. The video showed the unsteady, handheld camera recording of two apes in the jungle – but these are not like any other apes known to science. They had bodily colorations not before seen nor discovered. As for their behavior, the two apes were involved in a ritual that has got animal behaviorists baffled – each had their hands clasping the head of the other with their eyes closed as if communicating with one another via some meditative, telepathic means. Some behaviorists have compared the behavior to that of the Capuchin monkeys of Costa Rica, who have a bizarre ritual of holding their fingernails in the eye sockets of another. Speculation is that they do this as a sign of "trust" among one another. Some behaviorists have suggested it is a type of shared meditation and/or form of communication practiced by this new species of ape. Of course, there is a large contingency of persons who are dismissing the whole video discovery as a hoax, even though examination of the camera dates it to roughly 10 years ago. Who can blame them, with so many scientific hoaxes throughout history and the movie industry getting into the act with tales of "found footage" stories?

Along with the exciting discovery of this reclusive ape species is the intense investigation as to who the videographer was that filmed this rare video. In the news exposé, they show a picture of a young man, perhaps in his late 20s. According to accounts, he had 'disappeared' while doing entomological field studies in the remote jungles of Panama around the year 2007. As the TV is displaying the man's photo, Luis, laughing with Jorge and facing him, glances up at the TV and notices the image. He looks back at Jorge and jokes, "Hey, look at that guy! You probably looked just like that before you got married!" as he busts out laughing. Still laughing from the story Luis told before, Jorge turns to look at the TV. Still grinning, Jorge turns toward Luis, "Yeah, marriage will do this to ya!" as he dismisses the resemblance and continues joking with the other guys, who also notice the resemblance. As the guys are leaving the pub later that evening, Luis looks at Jorge and says, "I swear, Jorge, if you shave your beard, you'll look just like that guy on the news."

It is Saturday, and Jorge stays home for the day to watch over the boy as Alice is working at the hospital today. He and Carlos plan to watch a movie rental this evening of the comic-book blockbuster from several months ago. Until then, Jorge surfs the web and reads from his favorite tabloid news website. He sees the latest update to that found-video story. He now has time to get the full story and read more of the details. He sees that they have now identified the videographer as Brian Nunez, a contract entomologist from Pine Hills, Florida, just outside Orlando. He had just finished an assignment for a producer of a show about exotic insects due to air on the Animal Globe network. The producer said that Nunez had uploaded the commissioned clips, and they had already deposited their payment into Nunez's bank account. He figured Brian had gone on to other projects after not hearing from him for a while. When they tried to contact Nunez, they got no response and went on to a different contractor. Jorge scrolled down to the photo of Brian Nunez. As he contemplates the photo, he realizes why Luis made the comments he did. As long as Jorge can remember, he has always had his beard. Well, it was time to see what he looked like without it. Half an hour later, he emerges from the bathroom clean-shaven. Carlos looks up from his video gaming marathon, shakes his head, and exclaims, "Who the HELL are you? Jeez, you look like a different person!" Jorge picks up his phone and says to him, "C'mere… Do I look like this guy?" pointing to the photo of Brian Nunez on the screen. Carlos says, "Yeah, but this guy is a LOT younger and without your tan." "OK, thanks for the age jab," Jorge responds.

He begins to think, "Is it possible? Could this be me in my previous, forgotten life?" The earliest sentient memory he has is waking up in Granada, Nicaragua, about 10 years ago. That puts him near Costa Rica at the time of Nunez's disappearance. But why doesn't he remember ANYTHING before that? Upon reading deeper into the story, he realizes THIS is how he knows so much about the bugs and insects he has encountered. He *was* a scientist – an entomologist.

Jorge tells his wife about the realization. She: "What does it mean? What would they do to you? You know they'll deport you!" "Yeah, but if it is true and it IS me, I'm *already* an American."

He goes to the local authorities. "I think I'm this guy, Brian Nunez." "Get in line, pal. You're just the 100th person claiming to be him! Take a flyin'.." Jorge ends the call short. He looks up at Alice and says, "Obviously, the local authorities are not the ones to contact."

He calls a special phone number listed in a legit article seeking to locate Nunez. "Hello? I think I'm Brian Nunez. (pause) Wha?? OK. 'Oh my God, look at this one.' (pause, now with more emotion) 'Oh my God, look at this one!' On the other end of the line, an operator covers the receiver and yells across the room, "I think we've got him! 100% match on the voice print."

The FBI sets up a meeting place in the local Motel 6, not too far from Brian's house. He arrives with Alice, and introductions are made with the five agents there to meet him. While meeting with the feds, they show him 90 minutes of the video before the ape moment that was never shown to the public. Video recording of various exotic insects on the jungle floor and on the trees. Brian even mumbles the names of a few as they appear on the screen. After about 10 minutes into the video, the person filming says "Oh my God, look at this one!" while focusing on a new species of spider. Brian repeats, "Oh my God, look at this one". Spot on. He also sees the end of the video, which was also not shown in news clips - when the videographer yelps and the camera jerks away from the view of the apes, then the camera starts looking around for them again. A few minutes later, another yelp and the camera fall to the ground with just a rustling noise in the background.

"Does any of this jog your memory, Brian?" one of the interviewers asks. "No, nothing… just doesn't ring a bell," Brian says. After a long pause, "What about my family? Are my parents alive? And how about any brothers and sisters?"

They were prepared for this, and that's when they showed him photos of Roberto and Joselyn Nunez. They proceed to tell him that he was an only child and that his parents died in an auto accident the day before his disappearance. A drunk driver, while texting, veered into the oncoming traffic. He was just a kid. "Attempts were made to contact you, but voice messages and texts were not acknowledged," explained the female agent in the room. While looking at the photos of his parents, he doesn't even recognize he begins to sob, comforted by Alice. After a while, Brian looks up at the lead agent and asks, "Where do we go from here?"

"We've arranged, with your permission, of course, to meet with a world-renowned specialist in the field of 'lost memory retrieval,' Dr. Ivan Deiterman," the agent tells him. The methods of memory retrieval have vastly improved upon the time-tested hypnosis technique.

The next meeting is arranged at the office of a local psychologist who has offered his office for the session. In addition to Dr. Deiterman, Alice and three FBI agents are present. As he begins his first session, Brian looks acutely around the room, filled with countless artifacts (scientific, artistic, and religious). The therapist's office is a menagerie of items. He notices a framed display of butterflies on the wall. As he lies on the couch staring at the butterfly case, the drug begins taking effect. After a short while, he "awakes" in a memory…

He begins remembering chronological events in his life and describes them aloud:

- He is 8 years old, fascinated with a display case of butterflies and other insects;

- At 12, he started capturing insects in collection jars in the forest, examining them with reverence;

- At 15, he started his collection of insect display cases, covering the walls;

- At 16, he has his first girlfriend over, but she's freaked out over the live insects in his aquariums;

- At 18, he goes to college, certain of his career path as an entomologist;

- At 22, graduates, photos with folks, friends, GF;

- At 24, graduate studies in the field of photographing, filming;

- At 26, he begins freelance/contract fieldwork. GF is sad as he has to leave the country for weeks on end;

- At 27, he got his first iPhone - while purchasing, he set up an auto payment plan via his checking account;

- At 28, on assignment in Panama, wrapping up his commissioned work for Animal Globe, he is reading an article describing the hidden, undiscovered creatures of the remote Costa Rican jungles. Without telling anyone, he makes his way north to the neighboring country to do his own investigation.

Dr. Deiterman asks, "Brian, what do you remember about the day you disappeared?"

Brian begins to describe the incidents leading up to that fateful day.

It is early morning; he gets off a jeep, looks at his watch, and arranges a pickup time later in the evening. He ventures deep into the jungle, amazed by the species of creatures he sees – for him, this is *Candyland.* He walks along and discovers a tree that has a variety of insects racing and crawling on the bark. He spends several hours venturing through the jungle, filming for about 90 minutes the various species he observes. It has gotten to be late afternoon, and the sun is filtering into the forest at an angle, brightly illuminating incidental patches in the jungle. He figures he'll continue a little while longer, and then he will go to rendezvous with his ride back into town.

An exotic bird is heard in the distance, and Brian glances in the direction of the cawing. But instead of the bird, he notices in the branches about 40 feet away and 10 to 12 feet off the ground two apes of a species he does not recognize. At first, he has trouble focusing, so he quietly maneuvers to a better spot to observe. He focuses his video camera zoom in the direction of the apes. He can see that the apes are in sitting positions, facing one another. With eyes closed, each ape has his hands on the other's head, with the fingertips at the temples. It looks like they are engaged in some kind of mind-reading session. He is in awe of the splendid colorations of their fur – he's never seen anything like it before. Seemingly perfect camouflage for the jungle, with greens, greys, and browns. The only other primate he was aware of that had green fur was the Allen's Swamp Monkey.

Everyone at the session is sitting up and listening intently as THIS is the memory of the spellbinding video recording – and perhaps now the mysterious truth shall be revealed.

Brian continues: unbeknownst to him, a flying insect has landed on the back of his collar. It crawls up to his exposed neck and stings him. Brian lets out a yelp and instinctively slaps the back of his neck as he lowers the camera. The apes "wake up" to the noise and acutely look in the direction of the intruder. Brian quickly tries to re-establish the view of the apes with the camera, but they are gone. He searches all around, but no hide-nor-hair can be seen of them. After a few minutes, all of a sudden, something grabs both his arms violently as he yelps. The camera goes flying into the air and falls to the ground several feet away. He glances from side to side and notices two apes have grabbed and held his arms behind his back. The apes begin marching him in the general direction of where he had observed the two in the tree. He stumbles through the thick jungle as the apes direct his motion with their intent. They force him into an opening in the trunk of the large tree. One ape grabs him by the collar and pulls Brian, while the other is pushing from behind to get through a tight aperture.

The group at the hypnosis session are all listening intently, as this is what lies beyond the found video. The chief therapist is wringing his hands and thinking to himself, "I can make a career out of this guy!"

The two apes drag Brian down a corridor that suits the four-and-a-half-foot height of the apes but not so for a 6-foot human. Brian is at their mercy.

Despite being underground, the corridor is slightly illuminated by what appears to be phosphorescent crystals being held by other apes lined up on the sides of the corridor. The crystals seem to emit a green-blue light - some undiscovered material or crystal, perhaps? The two sentry apes lead Brian to a special chamber at the end of the corridor. Brian looks around the room as they enter. A large circular shape, probably 25 feet side-to-side and 8 feet high. The room is lit by natural light as there is a skylight/hole in the center ceiling, covered by translucent vegetation. The sentries stop Brian in the middle of the room. They take off his backpack and toss it off to the side. Around the walls of the room are various artifacts. Many are human in origin. There are some pieces from a small Cessna-like airplane that must have crashed in the jungle. Dread fills Brian as he notices a human skull amongst the items. Just back from the middle of the room is a primitive table about 12 feet wide with a rise in the middle, as if a podium. A figure from behind the table rises from the shadows, steps up onto a stump, and positions himself at the podium – a foot higher than the others. As he steps up and becomes more illuminated by the skylight, this is obviously the leader, Alpha-Male of the group. He seems bigger, older, and greyer than almost all the other apes and has an air of intelligence that sets him far apart from all the rest.

Brian, who is dumb-struck by the whole experience, is held about eight feet from the podium by the sentries. The leader motions two other apes from the sidelines to stand directly in front of the podium between himself and Brian. Brian can distinguish that THESE are the two he filmed in the tree due to the specific markings on their heads. The leader is quite upset at the two and lets out a series of grunts and screeches directed at them, accompanied by arm gestures. He eventually waves them to leave, with an added gesture implying, "I'll deal you two later!" The two sheepishly turn to leave, only glancing up momentarily at Brian.

As the leader directs his focus on the human, Brian begins to say, "Hello, my name…" Before he can finish, the sentries force him to his knees, and the leader leaps over the podium so as to be right in Brian's face. The Alpha-Male (AM) holds his hand over Brian's mouth to gesture, "Do not speak." The head-ape slowly steps back and falls into deep thought, rubbing his hand on his chin and cheeks, as a human would as if contemplating. As he slowly circles Brian and the sentries, he looks around as if to be searching for an answer. Then, as if a solution comes to him, he looks Brian in the eyes, reaches his hands to Brian's temples, and slowly does a telepathic engagement. After a moment, Brian seizes back as if jolted from a shock while the AM releases his hands from Brian's head. The ape has a shocked look on his face, with a dropped jaw and eyes wide open. He has seen something he's never seen before. He steps back with a distant look on his face while Brian is trying to regain his senses. Again, the AM falls into deep thought. The leader begins summoning other apes (who have begun gathering near the chamber entrance) to surround the human. The leader makes several gestures to the group of seven other apes (including the sentries) that they all understand. They all place their fingers on Brian's temples, with the leader then covering all their fingers in clasping of Brian's head. That's when it happens. Brian begins feeling a tingling with crackling noises in his head that quickly ramps up to shocks. Finally, he is jolted as if a bolt of lightning has struck him with a deafening crack. Everything flashes white, then to black.

He abruptly awakens from the session trance, weeping and looking for Alice. She rushes over and consoles him as they both are crying at the revelation. He feels as though he has experienced a tremendous catharsis. After calming him, she asks him, "What do I call you now, Jorge or Brian?" as they both cry and laugh at the same time. Everyone else in the room is looking at one another as if a mysterious truth has just been unveiled. Several in the group begin feverishly jotting down notes.

The therapist decides that is enough for this first session. Brian, having regained his composure, wants to see the notes of all the participants in the session. He insists on taking snapshots with his phone camera of everyone's notes, rationalizing that it will help him jog his memories of the episode. He is particularly interested to see how detailed he was in describing the events as he recalled them during his trance. They all agree to have a follow-up session to pick up from the pivotal shock treatment dealt to Brian by the new genus of apes.

After Brian and Alice leave the therapist's office, Alice looks at Brian and winks, "I got it all recorded," as she slyly pulls out her smartphone. Brian grins and gives her a big hug. She says, "See? I *told* you it wasn't aliens!" with a smirk.

News has leaked that Jorge *is* Brian Nunez, and the phone has been ringing off the hook with offers to do interviews and appear on talk shows.

At the follow-up session, little progress is made, as Brian cannot recall any of the memories "post cleansing," except for a couple of foggy memories of a "boat ride" and "washing dishes." They all agree to let Brian have some time to process the enormously cathartic shock experience.

TEN YEARS EARLIER

Just after Brian has been "telepathically cleansed" by the group of apes, he is left limp and incoherent, held up only by the two sentries. The AM thanks the group as they begin to disperse. He also gives them a brief, cautionary speech via pantomime before they exit the room. Once the room is cleared, the AM grunts and snorts at the sentries while making an odd dance gesture. The sentries understand and begin to drag Brian back out to the jungle. It is dusk outside, and the sentries dodge and weave quickly through the jungle thicket as they transport Brian to a new location. They have ventured for about an hour, and it is dark out now, except by the light of the full moon.

Soon, they arrive at the outskirts of a native compound. Most of the natives are dancing and chanting around a fire to the drums, making dancing motions very similar to what the AM demonstrated earlier. Out of sight from the natives, the sentries gesture to Brian to move forward toward the fire. Still totally zonked out and barely able to balance, he begins to slowly stumble towards the natives around the fire. The two sentries grin and quickly dash away silently. Several of the natives notice Brian and stop their revelry to stare at him, slowly staggering toward them. One by one, the natives halt their dance to take notice as the tribal drums slow and fade. Two of the younger native men begin to laugh at Brian's stupor condition as they approach him. One native grabs Brian's arm while the other continues to see if there is anyone behind Brian in the jungle but sees nothing. He comes back after noticing Brian is alone, and the two natives escort Brian to the group of natives. The group makes sport of Brian in his condition by laughing and making fun of him; he obviously poses no threat to them in this state. One of the natives says to the other, "Let's have him for dinner!" The other displays a maniacal face of happy approval.

Outside the jungle thicket, the taxi driver who agreed to pick up Brian at the rendezvous point has been waiting two hours past their appointed time. He looks at this watch, shrugs his shoulders, and gives up on waiting. He starts his jeep and returns to town.

Back in the leader's chamber, the AM is pacing around with a contemplative look. He knows it's not good that members of their group of apes have been observed by an outsider, and he's worried about that. He has seen humans before, and their reclusive group has stayed clear of observation for generations upon generations. As he is pacing back and forth, he notices off to the side the backpack the human was carrying. He suspects there are more human artifacts to add to his collection. He picks up the pack and brings it to the table. At first, he tries to pull it apart but quickly discovers it won't be that easy, being made of tough nylon. He notices the zipper and, after playing with it for a while, discovers its functionality. Even after he figured out how to open it, he plays with the zipper, back and forth, marveling at its functioning. He then spills the contents onto the table. Of the many items that tumble out, a flashlight hits the table and rolls across the edge, while a black case bounces off the table, falling under the table unnoticed. He quickly grabs the flashlight before it falls off the table edge. He examines it carefully and eventually clicks the lone button to turn it on. He is startled and drops it at first. He cautiously picks it up, realizing it won't hurt him. He becomes amused and runs around the underground compound, flashing it at the other apes, who are stunned and fascinated with the magical light stick.

Back at the native encampment, the natives are all feasting on their nightly meal and handing bits of meat and bread to Brian, who shovels the foodstuffs into his mouth. Brian continues to be in a stupor, slack-jawed and with eyes half open. The two natives who first engaged him are sitting next to him and laughing at his piggishness. They have 'adopted' Brian as their friend and watch over him. They remember a similar situation many years ago.

Later that evening, some of the tribe engages in spiritual practices with the use of a hallucinogenic drug. The two natives blow the drug smoke into Brian's face, who slowly falls back comically into an even deeper stupor. The next morning at the native camp, Brian is still in the realm of an infant mentality. Slack-jawed with a sleepy look, he clumsily mimics the ways of the natives by helping with activities. The tribe enjoys his company and considers him harmless. However, a couple of the elders are skeptical of the presence of an outsider in the tribe.

Meanwhile, with hands wringing and giddy anticipation, AM revisits the bag contents - still spilled onto the tabletop. AM is bubbling with anticipation, thinking of the next item to examine. He first toys around with a black ball cap with a Florida Marlins logo. He figures out that it is for the head and positions it on his head accordingly. He then picks up a pair of tube socks, examines them, and puts them over his hands and arms. He sniffs one of his sock hands and is taken aback by the foul smell. After he takes them off, he sniffs his fingers and notices they stink. He finds a tee shirt in the pile, sniffs, not bad, and rubs his hands on it as if a rag. He picks up a book entitled Entomologists' Field Guide and begins tactility examining it. He pages quickly through and sees the abundant photos. At one point, he is fooled by the realism of the insects and starts swatting at a picture of a wasp. He laughs and composes himself while realizing he has been fooled. He then starts admiring this object in his hand. He looks forward to showing it to the group. He picks up the notepad with Brian's notes and drawings on it. He examines and admires the sketches; he removes the pencil that is clipped to the tablet and examines the pencil… sharp tip, what for? Pokes at things… eventually, the pad of paper. Starts scribbling… gets refined, and draws a crude circle. But in his exuberance, he breaks the pencil; he puts it aside. He picks up a poncho, but he is attracted to what is underneath - a Swiss army knife.

The wise elders of the tribe explain to the two keepers of Brian that they need to take him to *his* kind across the "Great Lake" (Lago Nicaragua). The two get Brian, still brain-numb with a dumb expression, ready for his adventure, packing him foodstuffs and water to last several days. They row the large canoe across the scenic lake to the north side with a groggy Brian sitting in the middle. About halfway across the lake, Brian tilts his head back and stares off into the blue yonder. He begins to see kaleidoscopes in the sky. He leans way back and falls back into a daze. The native paddling in the rear says to the lead native, "Too much smoke for our boy last night." The lead rower laughs and says, "If I recall, you did the same thing your first time!" they both laugh. Once they reach the shore, the two lead Brian to a dirt road close to the docking point. Before sending him off, one of the natives gives him his necklace. They both point in one direction for Brian to follow, and he flatfootedly shuffles away. As the two head back to the canoe, they reminisce and joke about their fun time with Brian.

Back at the ape lair, AM is making his rounds in the den and checking with individual apes one-on-one. On two separate occasions, he greets two female apes and pats their pregnant bellies, no doubt his offspring on the way. With several of the other apes, he engages in the mind-meld sessions. Eventually, when he returns to his room, he hears some rustling in the room and finds the two sentries poking around the table. At first, AM is outraged that they came in without his permission and began poking in his stuff, but then he has an idea. AM puts the socks on his hands and does sock puppetry by mimicking the socks talking to one another. The two sentries are fascinated with the display, and AM gives a sock to each. They each eagerly put the sock on their arms and start mimicking one another while AM ushers them out of his room as if they were a couple of children. He smirks and shakes his head as the two walk away, enjoying their new toys. As AM walks back to the table, he sniffs his fingers again and makes a sour face over the smell. He returns to the table and proceeds to stuff all the items back into the sack.

After walking for several hours, Brian makes his way into the small barrio just outside of Granada, Nicaragua. He approaches several people, but he is still only able to grunt, so people shy away from the odd stranger. That night, he finds a place to sleep near other homeless people. The next morning, he finds his bag is gone, along with the foodstuff he had remaining. Later in the day, starting to become very hungry, he approaches a man taking a break outside a small eatery and begs for some food via gestures. The shop owner says, "I had to fire my dishwasher earlier; it may be your lucky day!" He realizes this person is a mute-in-need and gestures that he will give him food if he does dishwashing. After showing the mentally challenged man how to clean several of the dishes, he leaves him with a huge pile of dishes. Later that evening, Brian is savoring tortillas with rice and beans on the back porch of the small eatery.

Back at the ape camp, AM is setting up a large piece of an airplane tail as a makeshift door to his room, demonstrating a desire for privacy. He instructs the sentries that if they wish to have access, they need to make a scratching noise on the outside of the door – and WAIT for <u>him</u> to move aside the door. Later, he is back with the knapsack. Again, he spills the contents onto the table and discovers a couple of trail-mix bars. He examines the package, sniffs it, and tries to open one of the bars. After multiple attempts, he finds that pulling apart at the jagged end splits the packaging open. The trail-mix bar falls to the table. He carefully picks it up, already smelling its aroma. He takes a lick off it and beams. Then he takes a bite – Oh my! How delicious! After he finishes it, he grabs the second bar and is ready to rip it open; he pauses. Fighting the temptation, he puts it aside to save for later. He grabs the backpack and vigorously shakes it out to see if any more bars may be stuck in there. No such luck. He looks back at the second bar, again, fighting the temptation.

SEVERAL WEEKS LATER

Brian no longer has the slacked-jaw, stupor-look look, and he also has a scruffy beard now. He is beginning to recall some Spanish words as he reads signs and engages in brief conversations. The diner owner expresses his pleasure with Brian's attendance and hard work. Eventually, he asks, "My good helper, what is your name?" Brian, not knowing his own name, searches for something to say. He looks around and sees a political poster for a candidate named Jorge Perez and also sees the street sign for Gonzales

Avenida. "Jorge… Jorge Gonzales," he finally says. His boss jokes, "You seem to be getting your speech back… what happened to you? Did ya get abducted by aliens and get your brain wiped clean?" After a pause, Brian remarks, "Yeah, I think that's what happened." He hadn't thought about it much, but that seemed to be the only reasonable explanation for his condition.

The AM is sitting with his feet up on the table with the Florida cap on and is sharpening the pencil with the knife. Bored now that he's been through all the stuff in the bag and has no other 'toys' to discover, he is lazily toying with the flashlight, which is notably dimmer. As he is aimlessly shining the light around his room, he fumbles and drops the flashlight to the floor, and it shines under the table. It happens to illuminate an object. He discovers the black case that fell out unnoticed when he first spilled the contents onto the table. The case had tumbled to a shaded spot well out of the way of the view. AM picks it up and tries to open it. He finds it has a zipper device similar to the backpack. He unzips the zipper along the three sides of the case and slowly opens it. Inside, he finds a flat plate-like object about 4.5" x 2.5" x 0.5". Not much on it but one button, a couple of 'bumps' on the side, and a shiny emblem of an apple with a bite out of it on the other side. Along with it is a cube-like object with a long cord coming from it. Also, there is a long, thin Y-shaped cord. The AM has come across Brian's 1st generation iPhone, charger, and headphones that are in the case. AM senses there is something extra special about this item, probably because it has its own case and because of how enigmatic it appears. He carefully caresses the device, examining the several small buttons along the side. He begins pressing each button to see if anything happens. Finally, he presses the power button. He trembles as it begins to vibrate and light up. He gently places the device on the table and becomes mesmerized with wide eyes when the device begins powering up.

Brian has now made a routine of his dishwashing job and even has a small rental to call home now that the shop owner has begun to pay him with money along with the meals. On his way home after work, he has even ventured to stop into the bar and have a drink or two with several regulars. He doesn't talk much and mostly just takes it all in, occasionally adding a quip here and there. He stutters a lot at first, but with each visit, he becomes a little more fluent and confident with his speech and vocabulary.

AM has figured out the touch screen and is toying with some of the APPs on the phone. He has been able to figure some out, but most remain a mystery. He is particularly fascinated with the timer function. Using the pad and pencil, he has learned and written down the sequence of numbers 0 through 9. Later, he is teaching a class to a group of apes about this numbering system. Later, while alone and in his lair, AM is frustrated with a slow-running or non-functioning APP; he throws a mini-tantrum by swinging the phone dramatically as if to smash it on the ground – but he accidentally notices how when he raises the phone higher, it affects the signal, therefore the functioning and performance. He examines the phone closely, trying to figure out that a small sequence of vertical bars illuminate, one by one, the higher he holds it. He climbs on top of the table as close to the skylight and notices another bar is lit up. He tests his theory several times by lowering the phone and then raising it as high as he can to see the change in the signal bars. He ponders a moment, then grabs the iPhone and backpack along with pad and paper and heads out. He emerges outside and begins climbing his way to the tree tops, checking the signal symbol along the way. He settles at a comfortable spot near the top and sees that all five of the bars are illuminated. He begins trying and enjoying APPs he was unable to get to work previously. After a while, he just leans back and closes his eyes with a slight smile of satisfaction as he listens to a nice, mellow song using the Music app. He meditates with the sun on his face and a slight breeze through his fur.

Brian has become more and more cogent and begins to aspire to advance his livelihood. Several acquaintances suggest he visit the large capital city of Managua to seek out better opportunities. On his day off, he decides to take the 50 km bus ride from Granada to Managua. The bus ride is scenic, and he enjoys the thrill of adventure upon visiting a new place. Once in Managua, he picks up a discarded newspaper at the bus station and buys a coffee at a nearby café. He finds an available chair on the outside patio to enjoy the beautiful weather. He notices several positions for a dishwasher in the Help Wanted section and decides to check a few of them out just to get a taste of the opportunities in Managua. While sitting at the outdoor table at the café, a couple of women pass by and give Brian a subtle smile. The two pause and are about to ask Brian for the time when a flying bug lands on the newspaper. The two women are scared and quickly shuffle away. Brian is fascinated with the insect and declares its scientific name. He begins to say to the woman, "Hey look, it's an Umbonia crassicornis. Also known as the 'Thorn Bug'", but when he looks up, he doesn't notice that the woman has left. He thinks to himself, "Umbonia crassicornis? How the hell did I know that? " He carefully and without fear picks up the Thorn bug and safely puts it on a neighboring potted bush next to the café.

AM is depressed that his magical toy no longer powers up. He futilely presses the power-up button, thinking perhaps it is just "sleeping" or something, but to no avail. He had noticed a little rectangular symbol that kept getting smaller but didn't know what it meant. After sitting and thinking for a while, he looks at the case and dumps out the headphones and charger. He plugs both items into the appropriate holes of the phone, thinking that might make a difference, but nothing happens. Later, he has his head down on the table with the phone right in front of his face, contemplating the dead device.

He straightens up and has an idea. He pinches each tong of the charger with his fingers. After several attempts, he gets a spark that causes the phone to light up for just a moment but then goes black again. He ponders for a while and then calls in one of the sentries to assist. He tries pinching one prong while the sentry is pinching the other. Eureka! The phone begins powering up. AM starts grunting and screeching with excitement. The sentry is bewildered by the whole affair but knows it's a good thing when

AM is happy. After an hour, the two apes are sitting bored with their fingers still pinching the charger tongs, with AM letting out a yawn, followed by the sentry yawning. The battery indicator has only built up about 10% so far - but it is working!

SEVERAL YEARS LATER

Brian has settled in quite nicely in Managua. He works as a dishwasher at a respectable restaurant and also does part-time landscaping work with the day laborers on the weekends for extra cash. He is even living with a woman, Violeta. She is older than him but well-kept for her age. She exercises regularly and has a well-researched, healthy diet plan. Since he is living in her house, she is very controlling of his actions and is always after him to keep him orderly. However, he enjoys dropping in at the club to have beers with some of his friends.

One day at the club, on the TV, is a news story from the United States. It is broadcast in English but has Spanish closed captions for the locals. He finds it odd that he can understand English as well as he can. He jokes with the other patrons in the bar that he can understand English. One of the patrons exclaims, "You should get your ass up to America then, Amigo! The world is your oyster there." He gets particularly drunk that night and begins flirting with a young woman at the club. It's late, and Violeta goes looking for him and finds him being salacious towards several women patrons. They have a terrible argument, and she kicks him out of her condo.

AM has cleverly devised a charging setup that channels the electrical energy from multiple apes to charge the iPhone much more quickly. On the notepad, he has a crude drawing of the battery indicator that he has drawn large on the page, along with timing calculations for recharging based on so many apes participating in the process. On the other side of the room, several apes are engaged in recharging the lithium-ion batteries for the flashlight. They are told by the AM that time is up, and the one ape reloads the batteries into the flashlight. The ape holding the flashlight flashes the light at the others and screeches with joy as he runs out of the room, followed by several others who want to hold and play with the light stick. AM just smirks and shakes his head with amusement.

Brian now rents a room from one of his day laborer friends. He has also begun associating with a group that is planning to immigrate to California. It will cost him almost all his savings to do it. To him, it is worth it to attempt to live the dream of opportunity in the States. He is not comfortable with the shady characters that are organizing the immigration, but he figures if he knows a couple of the others going along with him, it'll be OK. First is the long road trip to Baja, California, in the cramped bus through Guatemala and the long, long trek through Mexico.

Once in Ensenada, they board a fishing boat packed with as many people as can fit. It is dusk as they plan to get to the shores of the California town of Long Beach by around 4 a.m. Once there, the group of 18 is quickly herded and crammed into a white van to be dropped off who-knows-where.

The ICE authorities have been monitoring this illegal immigration operation for some time, and they plan to squash it tonight.

The van begins driving towards central LA. After driving for a while, a siren is heard behind them. Everyone in the van has a sick feeling knowing that they've been busted. The van tries to elude the ICE patrol car as it swerves and bumps through the city streets, jostling everyone on board. Once they get a one-block separation, the van quickly makes a right turn, pulls to the side, and unloads all the people. They scatter as several patrol cars pull up and nab as many as they can. Brian gets away, running several blocks away down dark alleys until he runs into a group of three thugs while they are doing drugs. One looks up and says, "Well, lookie here… a wetback fresh off the boat! Come to take one of our jobs, asshole?" Before Brian can ask for help, the cruel thugs proceed to pummel him to a pulp. Badly beaten and bloodied, Brian manages to crawl to the street and collapse. A passer-by calls 911, and soon, an ambulance arrives to take Brian to a nearby hospital. Fortunately, they take him to a hospital that takes in indigent patients. He is admitted into the ICU when the nurse checks in on the comatose patient. Close inspection of the nurse's name tag reads "Alice."

AM has since devised an antenna for the iPhone to give better reception in the lair. He retrieved some coaxial cable from the Cessna wreckage and had it strung up through the wire meshing that constructs the skylight. He checks his signal strength, and now he can play YouTube videos down in the lair. AM is conducting lessons in his room, teaching a group about physics and science he has learned from watching YouTube videos. AM takes the airplane piece used for the door and converts it into a "chalkboard." He uses chunks of dirt as chalk, as he can wipe it off easily to clear the board. Later, he is seen drawing pictures of a group of apes. Several of the younger apes are horsing around, and AM has to get them in line - kids will be kids.

Several days later, Brian has fewer bandages on and is conscious. Alice asks, "Where you from, Mr. Gonzales?" as she looks at his name on the chart. "Nicaragua," he explains. She says, "Oh, so am I. Managua?" with a wry smile. He looks at her with a grin, "Why yes." She smiles broadly and says, "What a coincidence!" Later, the two of them are talking and joking. He explains that he does not know anyone here in the States, and she offers to help him, as she knows several expatriates. She does this because she has a sense he is a good and honest man.

AM and the group are having a good time as they are watching videos of "People doing stupid things" on YouTube. Several mimic the hilarious actions of the humans in the videos. Later, they are all quiet and frowning while watching "Apes doing funny things" – not so funny, eh? They watch the one where the chimp catches his own piss in its mouth. One of the smaller apes begins to chuckle, and all the others frown and glare at him. But after a moment, even AM begins to snicker, and before you know it, they're all laughing at the Ape videos.

Alice takes in Brian at her house to help him assimilate into the Los Angeles area. She introduces him to Carlos, her preteenager son. When alone with Alice, Brian explains in detail that he has no memories of the previous 10 years; he blames it on an alien abduction. Alice doesn't believe the story and rationalizes that he may have had severe head trauma before. She doesn't like him telling that story about the alien abduction and knows people will think him off his rocker for believing that. After several weeks, he has become comfortable with Alice and Carlos and has begun doing the day laborer thing at the nursery down the street.

AM is alone in his lair with the headphones on, listening to one of his favorite songs - Come A Long Way by Simple Minds. He is dancing to the music, with an obvious allusion to an Apple ad for the iPod with a silhouetted figure listening to music. Unbeknownst to him, several apes are just outside his door, peeking through the cracks and snickering at the sight. At the end of the song, there is silence, and he hears laughing. He rips off the headphones and swings open the door to find five or six apes snickering. At first, AM is very angry that they are laughing at him, but he settles down and begins to laugh with them. He then begins to share the experience of the headphones with each ape. Each has their funny dance moves, and the group has a hilarious time.

Jorge is in bed sleeping, well within the REM state, with eyes twitching rapidly. His REM continues to become more violent with contortions to the face. He dreams he is petrified in a spread-eagle position with electrical bolts converging to his head. He starts screaming, startling Alice. Brian wakes up sweating with a yelp. She comforts him and asks (in Spanish), "That same nightmare, hon?"

PRESENT DAY

They are flying Brian to the site where the camera was found. They land at the small airport in Los Chiles, Costa Rica, where a military hummer takes him to the edge of the jungle. They have cleared a path several hundred yards into the jungle to a spot precisely where the camera was found. There are soldiers all around guarding the way.

There is a news crew closely watching and chronicling every move that Brian makes. Two soldiers escort him to the exact point where the camera was found. Everyone wants to know if he can verify that this was the place where he filmed the original ape video and possibly provide any further clues to the location of the reclusive apes. Brian notices how they have gutted and cleared many of the trees in the vicinity in their efforts to find the lair of the reclusive neo-genus of primates. There is even an X on the ground nearby where the camera was found. Somehow, someway, he knows in his heart this is not the place where the fateful event happened to him – but he does not say a word. One of the leaders escorts Brian to a spot where they believe he was filming the video. He says to Brian, "We believe this is the tree you were filming the insects, and that tree over there is where you saw the apes," as he points off to the right. As Brian stands there with cameras pointed at him and filming, all he can think to himself is, "What if they *do* find them… what are they going to do to them?" After a moment, he looks at the leader, and the camera nearby points at him and says, "Yes, this <u>is</u> the spot. That's the tree I saw them in", pointing to the tree the researchers suspected. Very businesslike and without rebuttal, the scientific leader nods his head and gives a thumbs-up to a team of military officers and scientists standing by. The escort then retreats along with the cameraman to leave Brian standing there alone. Another representative from the military comes up to him and thanks him for coming here to verify the location.

OH, BTW- ABOUT EIGHT YEARS EARLIER

In the jungle thicket, two young Capuchin monkeys are playing with one another. One of them stumbles upon something in the loose soil. The monkey picks up what appears to be a dirty video camera. The two monkeys play keep-away with the fascinating, shiny object as they race to various locations in the jungle, taking it farther and farther away from its original location. A larger ape steals the camera away from one of the Capuchin monkeys and runs a long distance away to begin examining it. The ape stops, and after fumbling with the camera for a while, the ape is startled by a jaguar, drops the camera, and scurries off to join his shrewdness. The jaguar leaps in the direction of the ape and steps on the camera, planting it deeper into the moist soil as it runs after the ape. The ape uses his climbing skills to narrowly escape the jaguar attack.

Back in the present, we see many of the research team begin to leave the area of the found camera. Brian overhears a reporter in front of a camera explaining that they have speculated that the reclusive ape clan has either died off or has relocated elsewhere. From a high-angle, distant point of view, the hand of a camo-haired ape that is holding back leaves to spy on the retreating military and scientific personnel. The hand draws back to allow the leaves to obscure the view once again. He is wearing the familiar backpack. It is the AM.

Someone walks up to Brian and says, "You know you have the option to stay here as they continue to search for the apes' new domicile, Mr. Nunez."

After glancing around, Brian shakes his head. "If it still exists. Nah, I just want to get back to my family and let you guys do your job." He thinks to himself, "I really don't want to see them find the clan." It has been a whirlwind day, and he is exhausted as he boards the plane back to America. As he settles in the first-class seat they have given him, Brian decides this is a good time to go through the piles of emails and texts he has received for anything of personal value. Since this whole story has evolved, he has been getting talk show invites, offers for stories, and even a movie offer. He sees one from Alice and texts back to her, letting her know how it all went and that he'll be seeing her soon. He's super tired and soon falls asleep.

He arrives at LAX, and Alice is there to pick him up. They soon pull up to their gorgeous house, paid for by the substantial advance given to him for his book story. He is greeted by Carlos, who seems happy to see him again. He says, "We saw you on the news! But it looks like that might be the end of the story." Brian looks at them both and says, "I hope so son!" and gives Alice a long, tight hug.

Later that evening, while comfortably sitting in his modern, hi-tech office with the window facing the ocean, he decides to go through his countless text messages for anything of importance. He scans through until he gets this one. It came in during his Humvee ride back to the airport. He doesn't immediately recognize the number, but all it is is an emoji of a THUMBS UP. He dismisses it at first but soon returns to that text and scrutinizes the phone number closely. Why does it look familiar to him? He flashes back and realizes it's *his* old number – from ten years ago! His heart is racing with the thought that… no… that couldn't be - it's just a coincidence. Not knowing really what to do, he simply replies with a question mark and sets the phone down to get back to his autobiography.

After typing for a while, his phone indicates a message received. It's a text message from his old phone number. It has no text but does have two multimedia attachments. The first is a photo of him looking down at him in the jungle through the trees. He realizes this taken when he was trying to identify the location of the initial sighting from the video. He notices the hand of an ape with unique fur coloring holding back the leaves. His heart starts racing as he slowly opens the second image. His eyes widen, and a huge grin comes over his face. He then begins to laugh and sob with joy at the same time. It is a photo of a group of apes that have taken a selfie. Looming large in the center is AM, grinning with Brian's Florida Marlins cap on, along with two of his mates and four smaller children. In AM's left hand, he is holding an empty wrapper of a trail-mix bar.

END

PREFACE

This is a proposed story intended to be an episode for the show The Walking Dead. The names and characters supporting the main-introduced character can be changed with the intent to make this a stand-alone movie without reference directly to TWD. The story makes reference to "zombies", which TWD does not, therefore, uses of the word "zombie", Z, or Zs can be replaced with "walking dead", "walkers", etc.

Any semblance to the character or plot presented in this story, cannot be used without the expressed, written consent and agreement of the author.

LONE URBAN WARRIOR (LUW)

Introduction of Chopper Man

Bruce Clark Bennett - ©2020

Rick was leading his group into the city streets, looking for the building that was said to contain a stockpile of food. They had received this tip from a loner they had encountered in the rural area just outside of the city – just before he was devoured by a surprise group of zombies (previous episode of TWD). Zackary, they think his name was, had said to look for the "Humboldt" building and go to the 4th floor. This city is a reasonably large city with several high-rise buildings. Not knowing exactly where the Humboldt building is, the group wanders street by street in hopes of coming across the building's name. Spread out with a couple of lead scouts, the group hunts down the Humboldt.

All of a sudden, a couple of Zs spring out from behind a disabled truck. Eugene, surprised by the sudden attack, starts blasting with his 44 magnum he had recently found. The loud shots resonate off the buildings, and after a tense pause, Zs start pouring into the streets – from all sides. Seems many of the stores had Zs inside and were triggered by the loud noise of the gunshots. Several dozen Zs come around the corners, both in front of them and behind them. They're boxed in. The group huddles together in the middle of the street with Zs on all sides, absolute fear on their faces. (Commercial-break)

Then, out of nowhere, HE appears. They can barely make out his face with the hooded cape, but the rest of his outfit is all black leather, with some sort of tools or something dangling from his belt. He looks towards Rick and quickly says, "Take your group to that B-of-A building… and stay clear," pointing to the building behind the group. He then tosses Rick a key. Rick grabs the key mid-air and yells to the group to follow him as they take out a few Zs between them and the building. Rick gets to the front door and finds the padlock with a chain on the handles. He fumbles quickly to insert the key and glances up at the mysterious warrior but can barely see him from the hoard of Zs surrounding him. All he can see is a metallic, strobed glint as if metal is spinning rapidly and pieces of flesh flying around – mostly tops of heads. He gets the lock undone and scurries the group inside the building. As he gets the last of the group in, Rick gets the door closed just in time as multiple Zs crash against the doors. The members of the group move away from the clear glass doors, and each finds a spot behind the mirrored windows to watch the mysterious warrior. By this time, many of the Zs are heaped on the ground, decapitated, clearing the view enough to see the warrior at work. Some see him in slow motion, gracefully swinging the double samurais in a helicopter rotor motion.

The fully leather-clad character swings his device in such a way as to precisely slice the tops of the heads of the zombie hoard. He mows down row after row of the bloodthirsty creatures. Zooming out and in slow motion, this Z-killer's technique is marvelous, awe-inspiring, and just so freakin' cool.

The group within the building are all pressed against the windows, faces fixed and in awe over this spectacular warrior. Somebody says, "Is this guy for real?" A young teen boy exclaims, "He's like sumpin' out of a comic book!" A few instinctively nod their heads, but everyone is affixed to the windows, observing the hero. He's yelping and hollering to attract the Zs away from the building doors, who have given up on the humans that entered the B-of-A bldg… He proceeds to mow them down.

After leaving a pile of 3 or 4 dozen zombies on the ground, all missing the tops of their heads, things are calm and quiet. He stops his rotor blades by ditching them into the pile of bodies. He picks up his swords and, with a shred of a Z's clothing, wipes his blades off of the gooey flesh and blood. He undoes his rotor contraption and secures parts of it in a holster compartment of his belt (like some Batman tool). He removes his headgear, but he is not facing the building with Rick's group. He has long, shaggy hair and his outfit resembles an '80s rocker with his all-black leather outfit. The mystery man then puts away one of his samurai swords in this back sheath. He slowly walks around and pokes with his samurai into the heads of the few un-dead Zs that didn't get their heads sliced in half and still had brains intact.

The group begins murmuring to one another about the scene that has just unfolded in front of them.

Outside, our guy kneels down behind a pile of Z bodies and, hidden from view of the group in the building; he takes a severed "still alive" zombie head and allows it to bite & cling to the back of his lower leg near his ankle. He gets up and continues his search for moving Zs while having a decapitated head clinging to his leg – pretending not to notice. As people in the building notice the clinging head, he starts to hear rapping at the windows – trying to get him to notice. He begins to snicker to himself… "It worked." He looks up at the building and hears the rattling of large glass panes being pounded; he looks toward bldg and cups his hand to his ear as if to better hear them better. He looks down and around and acts like he is surprised by the discovery of the biting head on his leg. He nonchalantly raises his sword and swoops down on the head. BUT SOMETHING GOES WRONG! He drops his sword and raises his leg to hold his lower leg spastically. From within the building, everyone gasps, and some scream. One yells, "My God! He sliced his leg!!". After he hears the screams, he starts stumbling from laughing… he straightens up, shakes his head, and waves his hand as to say, no… no problem – just joking. The group in the building starts shaking their heads. A few are laughing, knowing now it was a prank, and others mutter, "What a jerk!" Everyone is astounded to see someone make LIGHT of a situation like this.

He calmly goes back to pick up his sword and anything else he may have left behind and starts walking toward the building. He wipes his blade on a scrap of clothing he rips off a corpse. As he's strolling toward the building, he sheds his leather jacket – exposing his leather vest and bare arms.. dude, this guy is cut, with toned arms and 6-pack abs (Chis Helmsworth type). One of the gawking girls who is smitten by him sees him strutting in slow motion. He looks like a lead singer from an 80s heavy metal rock group/ninja/superhero.

Just before the hero gets to the building door, he turns and looks around. Rick immediately sees that a Z is staggering towards him from 20 feet away. All the rest of the group, still with their faces pressed against the windows, simultaneously in union (comically), turn their heads to see what the hero is looking at. Hero reaches behind his back and pulls out a slingshot. He reaches down, picks up a stone from the ground, and loads his device. He pulls back on the sling and, when the Z is 5 feet away, lets it rip. The rock smashes into the forehead of the Z, pushing it back as it is stepping forward – comically, it balances for a moment with its front foot still in the air, then eventually falls over in a heap. Hero places the slingshot back behind his belt and calmly turns to enter the building.

As the loner-warrior comes up to the door, Rick and a couple of other hardened members have hands on their weapons, not knowing what to expect from this guy. Keeping eyes fixed on the hero, Daryl slightly turns toward Rick next to him and whispers, "What's… what is up with this guy?" Rick, looking at the hero, nods slightly and whispers back, "Just keep on guard."

The hero makes his entrance into the building. He looks around at everybody, grinning as he nods his head. "Hope I didn't freak out anybody too much with that little prank… I just knew I'd get you with it!" A couple of people in the group start to snicker but hold back when they glance at

Rick, who remains stone-faced, on guard, and focused on the outsider. He takes off his leather gloves and, along with his jacket and dual-sword-(cross) sheaths, places them on a nearby table. He unhooks a squashed but usable roll of duct tape from his belt. He holds it up to the group and says, "Don't leave home without it!" as if doing a commercial (that some of us know so well). Next, he takes off the policeman-type belt with multiple tools/weapons/devices dangling along the belt. Then he turns to the group, folds his arms, and comically says, "Well, don't all *Thank me* at ONCE!", spoken like some character from a movie. He immediately sports a handsome grin as several of the group step forward to shake his hand, pat him on the back, and say stuff like, "Thank you!" & "That was awesome!" & "How'd you learn to fight like that?"

The hero does a 360 spin, abruptly stops, and says, like the Beetlejuice character, "All right folks, nobody tries stealing my style, you know. I got a patent on that!" Then strikes an introspective pose and says, "At least I sent the paperwork to the government... " and then, with a serious look, scans the group and says ", But I'm still waiting for them to reply!" Several can't help but burst out laughing. Still, others are baffled and don't know what to think – looking around to see how others are reacting. Hero breaks into a grin and starts laughing with those who 'got it'. He says, "All right! So some of you SAW that show! Finally!" referring to some shared experience with a TV/Movie character.

Carol asks him, "What's your name?" This is when he goes into his routine. "Well, I'm a man of many names!" as an astute rogue from the 19th century. Yet in another character, "I kinda like the name Chopper Man!" laughing as he mimics this style – doing a chopping motion with both arms. "Then one time this chick called me the Lone Urban Warrior.. or 'LUW'… 'Lou'… 'L.U.W.'…' Louie'" each version spoken as a different character, "she even painted this for me" as he displays a slightly faded, 5-inch painted LUW logo on the lapel of his leather vest.

LUW goes around and meets each group member individually. Michonne, Abraham & Rosita, Eugene, Carl, Carol, etc. He makes a personal connection with each. He has a keen knack for 'reading' people immediately upon meeting them – no doubt a talent he acquired taking psych in college and working as a public servant for several years. When he meets Rosita, his eyes widen - he likes her. But he immediately senses Abe in his peripheral vision and, even without looking, senses his angry glare. He coolly looks at Abe and says, "Lucky man", as he encourages Abe to shake hands. Abe reluctantly gives a hand slap. He grins when meeting Michonne, noticing her samurai. He winks at her and says, "Ah, a girl after my own heart. Hopefully, we can talk more later on", as She reluctantly cracks a partial smirk.

He continues around the room…

As he meets Carl, Luw pulls out his slingshot and says, "Here, this comes in pretty handy… especially when you *run out of bullets*." he says in a sort of mocking way as he looks around at the group. Carl excitedly accepts and asks, "But don't you need it, ChopperMan?" LUW: "There's a sporting goods store 3 blocks away – I got more than I need."

LUW finally gets around to Daryl & Rick, who are sitting back away from the group and don't approach him. He can sense their fear and distrust. He knows. He's seen it all before. Again, adlibbing some show character, he looks at Daryl, who has his hand on his gun, and Luw chuckles and asks, "Well, are you gonna shoot me after I saved your asses??" Hero just grins and shakes his head. (This guy is like a cross between Robin Williams/Jim Carrey/Dennis Hopper.) "Man, you guys and YOUR GUNS!" shaking his head with eyes open wide and directed at Eugene. Eugene looks as guilty as a dog with his tail between his legs.

He goes back to his gear and pulls out a compressed, wrapped-up black vinyl bag. As he starts putting his gear in this bag, a couple of people close to him notice Z-teeth still sticking in the hero's cape before he stuffs it in a bag. He notices them looking and holds up the cape to display all the assorted teeth. He says, "Funny, this one time I took off my cape and found a full set of dentures clinging to the cape. I wish I could have seen the Z when that happened." (Quick, funny Flashback scene showing multiple Zs attacking the hero with an old hag Z biting down; it releases, with dentures clamped into the hero's cape.) he speaks to the group. "You know, I see two or three groups go through here a month. All types – you would believe what I've seen. But I can tell you guys are alright." He stops with his gear, looks around the group, and says, "You wanna know why? Because you have women… Not just 'cuz I like women (smirking & giving a debonair gesture) but because that means you folks still have some semblance of humanity left in you. It's those groups of all guys – they're like a pack of wolves. I nearly saw my own demise at the hands of creeps like those – I'm lucky to even be alive to talk about it with you today." Slowly shaking his head, a subtle pain comes across his face, thinking about it. (Quick teaser-flashback of him bound and imprisoned by thugs.)

Hero quickly changes the subject, claps his hands together, and asks, "OK, so… what brings you folks to this part of town? Just passing through?" He scans the room and looks for one to answer. As he scans around, he sets his focus on Rick. He gets a knowing grin on his face and slowly points toward Rick and says, "I think you're the leader." "As a matter of fact, I think your name is Slick… er.. no, Rick." All of a sudden, an excited expression comes over his face, and while nodding, he says, "Yeah, I've heard about you. Several people that have gone through here have mentioned you." "Tell me, whatever happened to the guy they called the *SENATOR*… no.. the *Governor*?" Rick says, "That's a long story. But he's dead. LUW: "Hope I can hear that story sometime."

Rick explains to LUW that someone told them there was a cache of food in the "Humboldt" building on the 4th floor. Hero says, "Yeah, I know the place. I can take you all there – it's outside my territory, so we'll have to be careful." He pauses for a moment and says, "Listen, it's late afternoon, just a couple hours light left… I can take you guys there now, or…" he pauses, looks around, then upwards. He straightens up and looks at the group, and says, "If you want, you all can be my guests, and we can party for a day…" pointing to the outside, "You all can FORGET about all this crappy nightmare for a day. I can take you guys to the Humboldt building in the morning – you don't want to be going there at night... I like you guys; I think we have some good stories to tell one another."

Rick, "What do you mean?"… Hero: "I mean, let's party!" Rick slowly looks around the group. Nearly all are nodding or giving thumbs up. A couple of them say, "Yeah!" & "Let's do it!"

Rick gives a cautious and subtle nod to the hero. Hero slaps his hands together and exclaims, "OK then… let's get this party started!" He strains his head & neck to see over the group to see the reception desk. "OK, we're in the Bank of America building… let's head up to the 3rd floor. That's where the goodies are. He turns to Rick and says, by the way, where's that key I tossed to you earlier?

Hero: "OK, let's lock it down here and head up the stairs. Somebody needs to secure the door."

LUW begins to ascend the stairs but abruptly turns to give his read of the riot act: "OK… we're gonna party and get lose a bit. But you get outta line or lose control, you're gonna get straightened out. Either by me or your boss!" as he looks over towards Rick.

As LUW leads them up the stairs, Rick & Daryl make sure the door is securely locked from the inside. Just then, Roberto comes running up from outside. He had gotten separated from the group just as they were entering the city. Daryl says, "Dude, we thought you were lost… what happened to you?" Roberto (17): "I was… I saw a place I thought might have some provisions. Turned out to be empty, but I lost you guys." Rick: "Well, you're just in time; we got a new friend that's going to treat us." Roberto enters, happy and relieved he has re-joined the group. They lock up the door and follow the rest of the group, who are already past floor 2 in the stairwell. They reach the stairwell door with the big "3" painted on it.

Hero brings them to a large reception/lounge area with lots of chairs and couches. There are several (6) small refrigerators along with a credenza with an amplifier and a bunch of iPods & phones. He says, "Check the fridges… got food, drinks & booze. Got a little pot over at that table. I'll start you off with a few tunes." He walks over to the iPods with a couple of young people from the group in tow.

Eugene from the group asks, "Where… er, how you getting POWER for this stuff??" Several of the group stand waiting for an answer while the rest descend on the fridges. "Well, when this Z-thing broke, I was holed up in some small tenement building – by then, everybody pretty much had turned or left the city. Aside from scrounging for food, I had a lot of time on my hands. There was a used bookstore a couple of doors down, and I found a book on generators. Plus, the internet was still working for a few months after V.E. Got that little building up and running within a week or so. But many of the newer ones," spreading his arms wide indicating THIS one, "have solar backup systems. It was a matter of getting them going." Carol, looking puzzled, asks, "Did you say 'Vee-Ee'?" Hero: "Yeah, V.E., Virus Epidemic. I don't know what you guys call it… the Plague?"

One person asked, "Where did you get all these iPods and phones?" Hero scuffs, "Are you kidding? They're all OVER the place. Remember before V.E. how everybody had their noses glued to their devices - when they should've been paying attention? They were the easiest targets for the walkers at first." He comically mimics someone obsessed with looking at their hand-held device and mockingly getting bitten by a Z. "Lots of good music on these things." I'm holding a couple of them up for people to see the contents. "This is one of my favorites", as he plugs one into an output jack to a speaker, and they hear a jamming rock tune. He starts rocking out, playing air guitar to a Joe Satriani riff – to a T. In the character of a gameshow host, he looks at the group and says, "If anyone can tell me the name of this artist, there is a fabulous door prize for you!"

After about an hour, everyone is loose and having a good time. Many are huddled around LUW as everyone shares stories of times before VE and harrowing moments once the virus spread. Quick cuts show various people describing and acting out past exploits, the majority of which are from ZUW, as everyone is interested in what he has been through and experienced.

LUW proceeds to tell the story of "The Bite". He unzips the left pant leg to show the teeth-mark scar. "When I got this one, I couldn't sleep for days." (Teaser for spin-off episode.)

Multiple scenes fade to LUW describing various adventures. LUW describes several different experiences, comically using pantomime for Zs. LUW encourages others to tell a story, and before you know it, most have a story to tell. This was a defining moment for the group as a whole, for everyone was relating and sharing at a level unparalleled before.

Someone asks ZUW, "What happens to all those rotting bodies out there on the street?". LUW looks at him and says, "Well, when you folks are on your way, I'll have a nice little weenie-roast. A good ol' bonfire ought to sanitize the place. You don't want a bunch of bodies rotting near the home. I remember the first couple times I did it; some Zs weren't fully dead yet," as he pantomimes a walker on fire, still approaching him, to the bemusement of the group.

It has become dusk outside, and LUW lowers the window louvers. All the time, he periodically goes over to the windows and does a quick check of the outdoors and street below. Occasionally, he disappears from the lounge area for a few minutes and returns to host the party.

While Hero is telling one of his many stories, he makes eye contact with Tara and gives her a quick wink. After a while, He and Tara are talking to one another. Roberto is seen in the background, eyeing the two, jealous of the hero's advances to Tara. He had been harboring a secret crush on Tara ever since he joined the group. Hero whispers something lengthy into her ear, and she lightens up but quickly quells her enthusiasm, not to be obvious to the rest of the group.

Hero walks by the group in discussion with stories. He says something to validate the speaker's story as he passes. He disappears and reemerges with another case of beer to put in the fridge. Several people get up and are more than willing to assist with the chore.

Abe & Rosita are bickering – no doubt Abe is harboring jealousy of their host.

At one point, one of the teens in the group members starts getting out of line. LUW graciously puts his arm around his neck and leads him to the window, whispering something into the teen's ear. The teen quietly re-joins the group, certainly more constrained and self-conscious. He'll be well-behaved from now on.

Later on, everyone is partying and having a good laugh. Even Rick and Daryl are joking about previous experiences years ago. (great scene) LUW and Tara are sharing an iPod with a Y-splitter, so they are both listening to the same tune. Tara is dancing and laughing as LUW is doing a wild air guitar in front of her. From his POV, he sees her grooving and laughing, and he's thinking, "Oh my God, she's heard this song before!.. and digging it!" From Tara's POV, she is watching him do his air guitar and is thinking, "I don't know WHAT he's doing, but I LOVE this guy!"

Several of the group are snoozing after a good deal of partying. Another couple (Glenn & Maggie) is making out. Hero jokingly says, "Hey, you two, get a room!" He kneels down and whispers to Glenn, "There's an office two doors on the left down that hall… a nice couch in there. And you can lock the door on the inside" as he winks at the both of them. They both have sleepy eyes and look at one another with drunken grins.

When he thinks no one is watching, the hero makes his way to a stairwell door and covertly motions (with a slight head nod) to Tara, who has kept a watchful eye on him. He slips through the door and is soon followed by Tara. Unnoticed, Roberto, pretending to sleep, gets up and stealthily follows from a distance. LUW grabs Tara's hand, and they go to the 4th-floor elevators. He has rigged the elevators to go down to the 4th only – not 1 through 3. After they enter the elevator and the door closes, Roberto emerges from peeking behind the stairwell door and runs over to where the elevators are. He frantically pushes the up button, but none of the other elevators work. He watches the elevator floor indicator of LUW & Tara's car. It stops on the 12th floor. Roberto registers the floor number as his eyes fill with rage. Up on the twelfth floor, the hero gently pulls Tara out before locking the elevator on the 12th floor. LUW embraces Tara, and they share a long, passionate kiss. Back down on the 4th floor, Roberto keeps pushing the elevator up-button, but the car is not moving from the 12th floor. After a time, he heads toward the stairwell. Meanwhile, the hero leads Tara to one of the executive VP's offices, complete with a super-modern washroom & shower. "Time for us to get squeaky clean, baby!" he & Tara giggle. Roberto is seen running up the stairwell. By the 9th floor, he is panting and exhausted but still determined. By the 11th floor, he is slowly proceeding up the stairs on all fours. Next, we see him exhaustively rapping on the floor-12 locked door and murmuring, "Tara… my Tara", with tears streaming down his face.

In the executive washroom, Tara, nude, in the huge shower, thinks she hears something in the distance, but then LUW turns on the shower and drowns out any sound she may have heard. He comes up from behind her and over her shoulder says, "Oh no… I'm turning!" in a Dracula voice. He begins to nibble on her neck as she starts giggling. His head descends out of camera view, and after a moment, she lets out a yelp of surprise and pleasure.

Meanwhile, back on floor 3, the party is winding down as the clock on the wall is nearing midnight. Many have passed out and are sleeping on cushions on the floor, most with grins on their faces. Even always-vigilant Rick can barely keep his eyes open. Daryl is fast out, having polished off a fifth of Southern Comfort. Rick groggily looks around and notices LUW is nowhere around. He gets up unbalanced and staggers for a few steps. He regains more composure and begins checking the other offices on the 3rd floor. He goes door-to-door trying the doorknobs. Most are open, and flip the lights on to see if anyone is there. He comes upon a locked door and begins to knock softly. Eventually, Glenn answers with a sleepy face. "Rick, wha… what's up?" Rick: "Just Maggie & you in there?" Glenn: "Yeah…

yeah, we're fine… wha'za matter?" Rick: "Nothing… just getting a head count. You go back to sleep", with a knowing grin.

LUW and Tara sneak into the main room where most everyone is sleeping on mats and comforters on the floor. Rick sees them from a distance and knows they've been up to something. He just grins and shakes his head before settling down for some shut-eye. LUW & Tara find an open space and snuggle on the floor. There is some nice ethereal music playing in the background. All is tranquil. (COMMERCIAL BREAK)

The ambient light of dawn slightly illuminates the main room, where all is quiet except for some light snoring going on. Abruptly, there is a crashing sound with banging on the stairwell door. Most of the group is jarred awake by the disturbing sound as they all look around sleepily at one another. LUW leaps up and heads towards the stairwell door with several of the group in tow. "Hold back this door", he yells to the small group that has followed him over. "I gotta see what happened!" as he heads quickly to an out-of-the-way room through a desolate office. Rick and Daryl follow right behind LUW. It is the security room, which has a single laptop on a lone table. He opens the lid and sees a quadrant of security camera views on the screen – two of which are of the 1st-floor lobby. LUW quickly scans the CCTV security recording. They see the hoard of Zs walking around the lobby - LUW mutters, "What the faa..?" as he's frowning. As he rewinds the video, each of them is wiping away the sleep from their eyes and trying to focus on the video. Daryl is squeezing his head to alleviate the hangover headache he has. In the background, the pounding at the door is still distinct, with group members talking, chattering, and yelling. LUW pulls the chair out and sits himself down. As they are scrubbing through the tape, they hit the point before the Zs came streaming through the doors. SOMEONE WENT ALONG AND OPENED THE DOORS. LUW slows the rewind to isolate the best view of the culprit and makes the video full-screen. It's grainy CCTV video, but just enough to make out who it is. It is Roberto.* "Who the HELL IS THIS!" LUW hollers. Rick & Daryl, in unison, exclaim, "It's Robbie…" LUW impatiently asks, "Why? Why the hell would he do this?" Both Rick and Daryl have bewildered expressions, and then Daryl "He's that new kid; he once told me he had a crush on Tara…" Rick does a painful sigh while looking upward while LUW groans, hangs his head in his hands, and starts rubbing his forehead with his fingers in a scrunching manner. He knows…. He knows why Robby did it. Daryl is all confused, spouting, "So what!? What does that matter?!" Before either Rick or LUW bothers to explain the details to him, LUW quickly gets up from the chair and rushes to the stairwell door. The Zs have managed to start breaking through the door with their continuous pounding. The only thing preventing them from coming in is the 4 or 5 group members pushing back against the door. With many gathered around him, LUW directs, "OK, I'm going down and make a racket to get them to retreat back down… and hopefully OUT of the building." Rick & Daryl volunteer to help in the plan to go with him.

Through a crack in the door, LUW jams a machete to slow the progress of the hoard behind the door. "Alright, just hold them back… we'll get them from behind," and he hands the machete to one of the other group members at the door. LUW goes to get his gear while Rick & Daryl arm up with weapons. As they start moving away, Daryl goes, "Hey, How are WE getting down??" LUW takes them to the elevators and inserts the key. Rick & Daryl look with their jaws dropped while LUW gives a "Well, what can I say" expression. As they are riding down, LUW is prepping his gear as Rick & Daryl glance at one another in admiration. LUW draws a quick, chicken-scratch map for Rick. "Here, in case we get separated". Rick looks at the note – 3-block west, 2 north. LUW: "That's where the Humboldt is." The three stand poised and ready to bail, waiting for the floor-1 bell to ding while the elevator music is playing (comical). LUW frowns and looks at the other two and says, "Wasn't this a heavy metal tune before?" On the first floor, LUW yells, "Let's get 'em, guys!" as the doors open and the men pile out of the elevator. There are a few Zs by the elevator, but they take them out easily. They briskly make their way to the stairwell. Once there, they slash & shoot the hoard while yelling to gain the attention of the ones on the upper levels. LUW kicks open the fire door going outside and draws them outside with his hollering and noise making.

Back on the 3rd floor, the door is just about broken down, but many Zs in the stairwell have retreated back down the stairs with the loud sounds from the lower floors. As the 4 or five Zs finally bust through the door, the group members are pushed back and race to claim a weapon to fight with. One of the Zs that busts through the door has Robbie's clothes on. Sure enough, it's him. Since he has recently turned, he is more powerful and quicker. He rumbles in and begins to lunge at Tara, who is 15 feet from the door. Someone off to the side skewers his head with a large blade. It is Michonne with one of her samurais as the lifeless body of Robbie falls inches from Tara's feet. Tara is sobbing as she recognizes Robbie.

LUW has managed to attract the attention of most of the Zs as he is back on the street. The stairwell is now clear of "live" Zs. Several of the group step over the dead Zs to get down. But a few of the group still on the 3rd floor are by the window watching LUW at a high-angle view. He finds himself in the middle of a hoard of Zs once again. Robbie had set up some noise makers to attract Zs from afar, so they were coming non-stop.

There is chaos at the point LUW was last seen. One Z has a samurai skewered through the upper part of its body. Several from the group had made it down to the street to try and assist LUW. Eugene starts blasting again with his .44 magnum and, after blowing off the heads of several Zs. He is startled by a Z that has grabbed onto his leg, and he begins to fall off-balance, still shooting. His gun unintentionally aims in the direction of LUW. A shot is fired that hits LUW's single samurai and (in super-slow motion) flies out of his grip – he is left with no sword. With Zs swarming on top of him, LUW pulls his leather face mask down and recoils while wrapping himself up with his full leather cloak. People watching from the 3rd-floor gasp in horror. Eventually, in the frenzy of the pile, a large piece of black leather is scraped up from the pile and moved aside by several of the Zs as they continue to ponce in the center of the pile. Several items from his belt are also tossed up out of the pile as they feverishly dig into the center of the pile of seething, ferocious Zs. He's a goner……He's gone.

The people at the window, including Tara, are horrified at the sight. Tara weeps as she and everyone else know LUW has been overpowered. She falls to her knees, pounding at the window. Her pounding weakens as she shrinks into a weeping bundle. The others at the window see Rick waving them down to head to the right (West). One person from the group tries to console Tara and eventually gets to get up and join the surviving group.

Rick watches LUW's plight from in front of the building in exasperation can't believe LUW has been killed. Rick looks down at the folded piece of paper in his pocket. It's a hand-drawn map showing where the Humboldt building is from the B-of-A building. He frantically gathers the group to get out of there. Eugene is tripped up and devoured by the spastic Zs.

The group runs to the next block, clear of the chaos in front of the B of A building. Someone cries toward Rick, "How did this happen!?"

Rick simply says, "It was Robbie". He turns toward the West and simply says, "Let's go." The rest of the group sporadically follows, some looking back towards B of A building, shaking their heads. Eventually, they are all on their way, but all are stunned and ashamed that they witnessed the demise of LUW.

(END OF EPISODE)

(NEXT EPISODE – THIRD ACT - ENCAPSULATED)

Rick and the group find their foodstuff and return the way they came. Many have knapsacks filled with food provisions obtained from the Humbolt building.

Once again, the group is surrounded by Zs - but this time, there is a narrow alley available that most can escape with free passage. Rick yells to the group: "You guys GO! We'll catch up to you." Several stay back and fend off the hoard. Rick, Daryl, Carl,… stay and fight the hoard. Things start getting out of hand as the three back up to the alley. Then, omg, it's LUW. Again, out of nowhere, he shows up whirling his rotor blades (or samurais in each hand), taking out dozens of Zs. Rick & Darryl look over at LUW, and each gets a disbelieving expression of relief while slightly shaking their heads. LUW yells, "You guys GO! I'll take it from here! – this is a walk in the park!" The swarm is diminished to just several staggering Zs. Carl, with the suppressed joy of seeing LUW alive, can't help himself from asking LUW: "How did you… what the…. How the hell did you SURVIVE?!" LUW glances over to Carl and says, "Rule number 3, bud. 'When in a swarm-street fight, do it over a manhole cover'' (Could have a quick flashback here of escape, or save for Episode.) With a grin, he looks back and decapitates several more Zs. Carl: "What's rule number 1?" LUW looks at him with an "are-you-kidding-me" expression and says, "Don't get bit!" Carl: "What's #2?" LUW chuckles and says, "Next time, little dude," as he finishes off a couple more Zs. Rick comes over to Carl, grabs him by the shirt, and leads him toward the alley. Rick looks at LUW and gives him a slight nod of thanks as he, Carl, and Daryl start jogging down the alley. LUW shouts to them from 100 feet away, "I'M SENDING YOU GUYS

THE BILL FOR THE CLEAN UP!" Rick & Daryl exchange muted grins and keep running to the rest of the group.

After some time, the three catch up to the rest of the group. Out of breath, Daryl and Carl explain that LUW is still alive and helped them escape. Tara, hearing this, lights up and bristles with emotion. She begins to motion back to the city but is held back by several in the group. As she's sobbing, they explain to her that he's a loner and that she would be killed if she tried to join him. After some consoling, she accepts their reasoning, and the group moves on.

END

Flyby Swap

Sci-fi, Adventure, Comedy

Bruce Bennett – ©2020

A young man sits contemplatively in the disheveled, dark room, looking out a large picture window while smoking a cigarette. Books are stacked on the tables, and papers are strewn about. He thinks to himself, "I never really believed in much of the metaphysical stuff that was thrown around. The idea of ghosts, multiple universes, telekinesis, mind-out-body experiences, even UFOs and alien abductions – that is, until about a year ago. Despite my vivid recollection, I'm still trying to wrap my head around it, but I'll do my best to explain what happened. Here is my story…"

One Year Ago

It was Saturday at 6:15 AM, and I was walking towards the kitchen to get my morning *spark*. As I was preparing the dark-roast ground coffee for the coffee maker, placing the filter, and adding the water, nature called, and I had to take a piss… badly. I was dancing around, getting the water into the machine and pressing the brew button. I quickly raced to the bathroom to finally relieve myself. As I was standing there, while taking good aim, I began to have the most unusual sensation. My body began to tremble, and my head started spinning. My stream began going all over the place, and I heard a gradually increasing swooshing sound.

Then, everything turned black… and silent.

When I came to, it was dark, and I couldn't see anything. All I could hear was the soft murmur of electronics with low resonance oscillation. My body felt very weird – not bad or painful, just very unusual; a discombobulated feeling. My sight slowly began to come back, starting with a fuzzy blur. The first thing I tried to focus on was my hands, which felt odd. These were not my hands, nor the hands of a human at that. My flesh was green-blue, and the digits, 6 on each 'hand', resembled that of a frog or amphibian. My 'fingers' were long and flexible, with a suction cup at the end of each digit. I could even fluctuate the size of the suction cups to 3 times their size and down to almost a sharp point. When I would bring the tips of my fingers together from opposite hands, the tips would fuse – this also 'centered' and balanced me. This was so fascinating that I spent several moments playing with this phenomenon. There seemed to be no bones in my arms, but they were rather like the trunk of an elephant. As I looked more downward, I could see my body did not split into two legs, but my torso extended to the ground and feathered outwards with tentacles that were of a silver tone. I began to feel my heart beating more pronouncedly. Finally, I slowly looked upward and found 2 strange and fascinating creatures standing in front of me. Resembling nothing I have ever seen on earth – or could even imagine. My heart began racing. I saw that each creature had 2 sets of upper limbs. I found I was able to swivel my head a full 180 degrees to discover that I, too, had 4 upper limbs. I turned back toward the two creatures, and it hit me that I was *one of them*. I looked at their faces and instinctively started touching my face to feel the three round, black eyes situated in a triangular pattern - this explained the acute 3D depth perception I now have. Above the eyes, I felt the 3 horizontal slits – one in the center of my 'forehead,' flanked by a slit on either side. I could sense that these were nostrils for breathing. Below my eyes, I felt a circular indentation – kind of a bowed, inward bevel - where one would expect the mouth; no orifice or opening – just a soft spot where the outer skin bowed inward. I tried to say something, but nothing sounded, which made me think this was not any feature to communicate with. With my heart still racing, I began to become light-headed and unsteady. I began to faint and fall forward towards my captors/hosts. I instinctively raised my two front arms to break my fall, but one of the aliens reached out, and our fingertips came together and 'fused' at the fingertips. I felt an incredible sensation that seemed to calm me and re-establish my orientation and balance. My heart seemed to be at ease, and I felt a wellness in my being. As I straightened up, my fingers detached from the alien. For a long moment, we all just looked at one another silently.

Again, I instinctively tried to speak by saying, "Where am I?" but nothing sounded. That's when I was struck by the realization that communication was done telepathically rather than verbally.

That is when they began telling me who they were, where I was… and why.

They called themselves Vanguardians from a planet in the galaxy humans refer to as the Sagittarius Dwarf Galaxy, some 65,000 light years away.

And I was on their space-folding hyperspace ship. Seems they have mapped numerous worm-holes around Sagittarius Dwarf and have mastered the ability to utilize the worm-holes – with predictable results.

The two introduced themselves to me. One was named Ti'desect, and the other Stuwaskilivary. When I suggested calling them "Ty" and "Stu," they looked at one another and made a high-pitched, trilling sound that I perceived as laughter.

Ty said, "That is quite all right; you can call me 'Ty' and my associate 'Stu' if that will assist you in your communication with us. And what do we call you?"

I said, "My name is Alexander Rivera Koenig, but you can call me Alex."

They both practiced saying the name. At first, slowly and deliberately, and then more quickly and assuredly.

They went on to describe that they do this type of 'consciousness transference' experiment with each and every 'intelligent' civilization that they come across in their travels. The mental swap lasts for a period of one local global rotation, so in my case, it will be for 24 hours. I felt a wave of relief, knowing that this was only a temporary experience and I would soon be back in my human body again.

They were very polite and even apologetic for causing this disruption in my daily routine. They assured me that I would find this to be a tremendous and enlightening experience - one that I would delight in sharing with my fellow humans. It crossed my mind to ask who I was 'swapped' with, but I was immediately distracted when Ty held up a small device.

With the small hand-held device, Ty then began projecting holographical graphics and videos into the dark atmosphere as a teaching aid. I was awestruck by the technology - how they could project visuals that were 20 to 25 feet in height, that is, if I were 6 feet tall - I had no sense of measurement and no reference available. They must have 'heard' me because they projected a human figure next to me, and it came less than half my height. So, I figured my alien body was about 12 to 13 feet in height.

They showed me holographically the dozens of other species they have done this with. I was astonished to see other alien races they had come in contact with. I felt like I was in a cross between a Star Wars movie and an HP Lovecraft story. They were lined up, and Stu said they were in the order of development of higher realms such as intelligence, society, technology, etc. Ty pops a 3D holograph of a Vanguardian at the front of the line as he leans in towards me and whispers, "Well, you know… we _are_ at the top of the list."

Of course, I couldn't help but ask, "Where would you put humans on this ranking?"

Ty and Stu look at one another, and Ty presses a button on his remote, and all the alien figures shrink to 30%, and a hundred more figures line up at the lower end. A human figure is hovering above the alien line and descends way back to around 120th place. They begin inserting the human hologram behind an upright rodent-looking creature resembling a raccoon.

Astonished, I blurted, "REALLY?!"

Ty and Stu slowly looked at each other, "No, NOT really… we're just kidding!" and they both trilled loudly as they repositioned the human to about 14th place. At least Vanguardians have a sense of humor.

Once their trilling calmed down, they went on to mention that they've even tried the transferences with non-intelligent life but quickly discovered it was far too dangerous, and the risk of losing the transferred subject proved to be too high, so they abandoned that study.

They proceeded to describe and display how they had advanced their interstellar travel to light speed for some time now and were charting a new hyper-warp path to the Andromeda galaxy when they realized they were going to traverse the galaxy known to Earthlings as the Milky Way – and so happen to pass through the solar system containing the planet Earth. They have developed advanced sensing devices to detect planets with life – so the Earth had popped up on their 'radar.' At 150 light years away, they captured our earliest broadcast signals and, shortly after, were able to decipher a knowledge base for our species.

I finally had to ask, "But of all the billions of humans on Earth, why did you pick me? Specifically, me?" They explained that it was totally random that I was the subject of their consciousness-swap experiment. It had something to do with the fact that I, specifically, was in the exact, perpendicular coincidence of their alignment with Earth and their ship at the moment of transference initiation. A nanosecond later, and it would have been someone else. Guess it was just my lucky day.

I amused my hosts by telling them that an Earthling had written a story about an alien race seeking a new hyperspace bypass, and in the story, the traveling beings obliterated the Earth because it was in the WAY of their new pathway. Once again, they began trilling; they found that amusing because they would NEVER, EVER consider doing such a thing. Life is sacred, regardless of its development. To the Vanguardians, it would be inconceivable to destroy life so indiscriminately.

I asked, "How long did it take for Vanguardians to achieve their level of advancement?" Ty and Stu looked at one another, and Ty projected a calculator displaying their numbering system to convert Earthling's time to their system of time measurement. After several calculations, Stu proclaims, "In about 2.7351 million of your earth years."

They began showing me many aspects of their science and technology, along with their system of government and social structure. Soon, they went into depth describing their cultural and philosophical tenants. The Vanguardians had the benefit of accumulated knowledge and wisdom of dozens of intelligent species and could pragmatically glean the best attributes from each.

Medically, many of their biological systems are based on a triad configuration; both the heart and brain have 3 lobes. Ty rambled on about the neurological configuration and how their species were able to completely master the control of their thought processing – it went way beyond my Psych 101 knowledge.

They explained that I was not breathing air as I know it from the earth, but rather an ammonia-based gas native to their planet. They went on to describe other conditions of their anatomy and activities.

I couldn't help by constantly thinking how I wished I could record this conversation. So much was going over my head. So much to tell my human contemporaries.

We talked for hours and discussed a myriad of topics, including:

- Evolution of species - their caution to humanity for our unbridled extrapolation.

- Mass extinction – how they survived theirs; I told how we were into our 6th.

- Other Alien Races – what they've learned best.

- Maladies plaguing Earth - they suggested their solutions.

- Wars – they have no such concept.

- Trash and Waste.

- Epidemics.

After hours and hours of discussions, I began feeling very tired, and I do believe I even dozed off a couple of times, and they didn't even notice. Boy, how handy that would have been in my school days. Eventually, they offered to have a meal, and that woke me up considerably. We had a wonderful dinner of their native food. However, I had to avoid looking at the cuisine, as it would be disgusting to a human. They had to show me how to consume it – it was ingested via an orifice-sphincter in the center of the tentacle hands. We would just squish it between our hands. That was bizarre.

We were on the 24th hour of my stay, and we began exchanging pleasantries for my departure. I was already retracing my remarkable experience with my gracious hosts. As the time was winding down to the last minute, I thought to ask, "So the individual you got to swap with me, is this person a scientist? Doctor? Sociologist, Philosopher?

Stu says, "Well, because we were already en route, we didn't have much time to prepare for the swap, so we sought a volunteer. We got someone from the maintenance department. We only later found out he can be somewhat of a rascal. His name is D'gorion."

Before I could even respond to what he said, my body began to tremble and shake. I could barely make out their gesture for 'farewell.'

After a moment, D'gorian was back in his body. He immediately slumped over but fused his fingertips and slowly retained his proper, erect posture. He quickly examined his body. When D'gorian realized he was back in his own body, he began loudly trilling and exhibited signs of immense joy and merriment – rarely is this seen in a Vanguardian by nature. He began flailing his arms above his head and danced past Stu and Ty. For a moment, the two were shocked at D'gorian's behavior, but then Ty turned towards D'gorian, extended his arms as to suggest 'come back here,' and said, "But D'gorian, we need to debrief you!" Ty and Stu remained baffled as D'gorian continued to dance away.

Sunday 6:15 am – My Earthly Return

Back on Earth, I became reunited with my human body. I immediately felt a surge of electricity shoot through my body. Then, the pain started to creep in. The pain was felt all over. The first pain to take center stage was my groin – it felt like I'd been kicked in the nuts. This made me bend over and put my hands on my knees to steady myself and reduce the weight on my hips and torso. I saw that my hands were bruised, and my knuckles were red and raw. And my crotch was all wet – did I piss my pants? I looked up with my blurry vision to see where I was and could see I was in my hallway, headed for the bedroom. I assumed I was trying to get to bed because of the immense exhaustion I was feeling. As I staggered into my bedroom, I glanced at the mirror and could see my face was bruised and scraped up, and with two black eyes. Something was on the side of my face – I think it was dried vomit. I went closer to the mirror to examine the facial damage. I had that awful taste of blood in my mouth. Slowly and with much trepidation, I opened my mouth to see how many teeth I might be missing. With great relief, I found no teeth missing or chipped. But that relief was short-lived. I lunged onto the bed – even *that* hurt.

As I lay there, I could only think, "What the hell did D'gorion do while he was here?" I would begin twitching from each pain that decided to take center stage. I looked over at the bedside table and noticed my phone. The front face was cracked and shattered at the corner. I noticed I had dozens of messages, quite a change from the usual 3 or 4 that I get during 24 hours. I opened the messaging app with the same trepidation as I did when I checked my teeth. The first message was from my girlfriend, Jenny… I suppose that said it all: "YOU F*CKING MORON! HOW COULD YOU DO THAT???" The rest of the messages weren't so nice. "Dude! I'm gonna SOOOO punch you next time I see you, dickhead!" – that was from my buddy Bill; "Did I kick you in the BALLS hard enuf!?!?" – That was from my best friend, Darren. Jason was a bit more descriptive, "THX for getting us kicked out of our favorite strip club! Now, where are we gonna go to get 2-for-20???" A couple of other friends simply put, "Alex- U A-hole." After about eight, I couldn't read anymore. I could only think, is my life ruined?

The pain in my head began to match that of my body. Thank god there were a couple of pain-killer pills next to my bed because I was too exhausted and hurting to try to get up to go to the bathroom. Fortunately, the drugs took effect quickly, and I was out like a light.

I was able to get several hours of sleep. I dreamed of my fantastic visit with the new alien friends but soon woke up to my ugly reality.

I went through my voicemails but could only go through a few. It was worse than the text messages because you could *hear* the anger and disdain in their voices. I feared listening to the one from the LAPD. I'll save that for later – just can't handle that one now.

I watched several video clips others had taken of me being an asshole or moron. Jenny videoed me, or should I say D'gorion, using his Vanguardian logic to constantly argue with her regarding just about everything – and, of course, that NEVER goes well. Darren had a clip of me downing way too many shots. Several others made reference to *that* video. I didn't know what they were talking about, and frankly, at that point, I really didn't *want* to know. But…

Then I saw ***that*** video.

It was taken by Gilbert during our strip club venture. Gil hadn't sent me any inflammatory messages - he probably was just glad it wasn't himself being the total ass this time. It was a low-angle shot of some guy up on the stripper stage from behind; the light was behind the figure, which mostly silhouetted the guy, but there was no mistaking it was me. My trousers were halfway down my thighs with my left hand raised high, flailing like a cowboy on a bronco. My right arm was making a jerking motion, well, in that area. Geez, I was jerking off on stage? In front of the stripper and everybody there? It didn't last long as two big bouncers grabbed me and yanked me off the stage. The video ends abruptly, as if the bouncers swatted the camera out of Gil's hands.

Well, that there explained my physical condition.

That was enough for now. I downed a couple more painkillers, and as I lay there, wishing only to return to the alien ship – and perhaps start a new life as a Vanguardian… and find that D'gorian.

Then, I got a call from my mom. Alas, a supporting voice. I answered with much relief, "Oh, Mom, I'm glad to hear from you. I've got something to tell yo…"

"Are you trying to get disowned?!" She hollered. "Don't let me EVER see you on TV like that again!" CLICK. My stomach began churning just thinking about what THAT might have been about.

The more I pieced together D'gorion's shenanigans, the more I realized he indulged in 24 hours of unbridled hedonism. If I could only get face-to-face with him, I'd strangle him. But… he is probably millions of miles away now – literally.

I decided to take a couple of days off from work to get my life back together. Thank god my bosses hadn't caught wind of my escapades - at least not yet. I could only pray I still had a job when I returned.

Days later, it was difficult, but I began reaching out to several of my closest friends to explain, but, of course, nobody believed my story. Who would? Many didn't even want to talk to me. I ended up leaving a lot of apologetic messages. The most popular reply was: "You've got a lot of nerve!"

I even conducted my own intervention to gather those I had offended to apologize - and try to explain. I knew my story would not be easily received. Half the people just walked out. The ones that stayed just sat with arms folded and angry frowns.

* * *

After several months, I gradually reestablished many of my closest relationships. Jenny, Darren, Bill – they all eventually 'took me back' - albeit cautiously and with guarded reserve. The whole incident was 'written off' as a temporary insanity - thankfully, without legal entanglement – with a promise that it will never happen again. Although my mom took the longest to reconcile with – she certainly did NOT want to admit to any 'insanity' in the family.

Saturday – 6:15 AM – Earth – That Fateful Day

D'gorion arrives in the human host, wobbling as he balances himself. He is standing with a wide open robe while in the middle of urinating. He's startled at first but soon realizes that he is in the middle of a bodily process of eliminating toxins and wastes from the body. He catches on quickly that the toilet is the target. But this is not a sensation in the repertoire of a Vanguardian – a sensation of bodily RELIEF and pleasure from the process. Even when done pissing, he stands there for several minutes examining the new host body he occupies. How strange it is. He is startled by a ringing noise going off, and he looks down and around. He discovers the sound coming from his left side and finds a hand-held device in the pocket of the robe. He has discovered Alex's cellphone. He doesn't know exactly what to do, but after a couple of taps, he happens to press the green answer button. It's Darren, "Hey Alex, catch the strip club tonight?" Willing to participate, he says, "Yes, I will join you." Darren replies, "Cool! Pick you up at 8 tonight." The call ends, and D'gorion begins playing with the fascinating handheld device he has. He comes across the Gallery and laughs with a slight trilling sound at some of the humorous images. He becomes mesmerized when watching several video clips. He is still standing there at the commode when he initiates a porno clip. Then, he feels something 'moving' below. His eyes bulge as he sees a part of his anatomy grow at such a quick and expansive rate. He reaches down with his right hand to examine if the member is okay. D'gorion soon discovers a sensation unknown to a Vanguardian. He proceeded to pleasure himself, and at the moment of orgasmic ecstasy, Jenny, wearing only an XL tee shirt, opened the bathroom door, frowned, and said, "What the hell you doing?" He drops the phone, shattering the glass face at the corner - setting the stage for the next 24 hours.

* * *

Once again, the man is smoking a cigarette. "Well, that's my story; take it or leave it."

Just then, Jenny barges into the room and flips on the light, "Hey buddy, you gonna miss your party!?" She looks around at his cluttered office and says, "Honestly, I don't know why you like your office so disheveled like this."

"It gives me perspective," he says dryly as he puts out his cigarette and gets up. A picture he had on his lap falls to the floor. It is an illustration of a Vanguardian with a gun crosshair overlaid and the name D'gorian scrawled on the bottom.

As Alex follows Jenny into the well-lit living room, a dozen people are celebrating with a banner draped on the wall: "CONGRATS ON THE BOOK DEAL AND THE <u>HUGO AWARD</u>!"

The young man turns to the audience and says, "If they don't believe you, make it a FICTION!" with a wink.

THE END

Inside-Out Tee

(Skull-tee)

A Horror Farce

Bruce Clark Bennett - ©2020

RICKY

Ricky works at the Xchng, a hipster, used clothing store near the university in a Los Angeles suburb. He's been there for about a year now. It's not his first choice, but there are slim pickings for a Communications major, even with a 4-year college degree. Coupled with a crappy economy, he, like many others in the same boat, takes what they can get. Ricky is one of those Boomerang-Generation young people who have moved back to their parent's home for economic reasons.

At the Xchng, he makes the most of it. He enjoys the customer interaction, plus he gets first dibs on many of the clothes that are brought in for exchange. His thing is tee shirts – he has quite a collection at home, much to his folk's dismay. A couple of times, he has even sold the shirt off his back to a customer that wanted his particular tee shirt. He once got a hundred dollars for a hard-to-find tee he had on – nice profit for a $15 tee.

The Xchng just hired a new guy, Sean. He and Ricky hit it off right away, as Sean shares the same useless degree and Boomerang status. After a few days of sharing stories, Sean invites Ricky to his parent's house to play some basketball and video games. They both have Tuesdays off, so they plan on that day.

Tuesday rolls around, and Ricky wakes up at 10 am after binging much of the night with the latest popular TV show – some spooky one about a haunted house. He looks in his closet to pick a tee shirt to wear. He at first thinks to wear one of his "special tees" to impress Sean but opts for a "throwaway" tee since he'll be playing basketball. He grabs one from his "rag" stack, a black shirt with a simple, comical, slightly grinning skull. He sniffs the armpits to make sure it's okay and puts it on. For a couple of months several years ago, it used to be one of his favorites until he started working at the Xchng, where he has since picked up countless cooler tees.

Ricky grabs a microwavable breakfast burrito, does a quick heat, hops into his rundown Camry, and heads to Sean's while munching his food. He arrives at Sean's house around 11 a.m. Sean answers the door, munching on one of the same burritos that Ricky had just eaten. Ricky laughs and says, "Yeah, I love those things!"

Sean gives Ricky the nickel tour of this folk's house, pausing by the room of Sean's sister, Samantha, who is off to college. When he opens the door, there is an ominous gloom in the abode. Seeing Ricky reaction, Sean says, "Yeah, she got into some weird shit her last couple years of high school… black arts, mysticism, the occult. She became one of those *Goths*, though she's getting back to normal in college."

Ricky quips, "What is her major? Witchcraft?"

Sean chuckles, "No, accounting… she wised up and decided to get a *useful* major… unlike us, eh?" Sean gets to his messy room and grabs his basketball. Soon, they are heading to the nearby park with a B-Ball court.

At the court, there are two other young guys already playing. Ricky and Sean watch them playing one-on-one for a bit before going over and challenging them to some two-on-two. They play shirts and skins. Ricky and Sean choose to be skins, then pull off their tee shirts and begin playing. After a brisk workout of three games, the guys shake hands with their opponents, grab their shirts, and head back to Sean's, topless – soaking in the sun on a warm summer day.

Sean goes, "Not too bad, 1 out of 3… for a first time".

Ricky replies, "Yeah, we'll get better. I'm a bit rusty. Next time, TWO out-of-3," as they fist-bump on the way home while wiping some sweat from their brow with their shirts.

When they get inside the house, Sean says, "There's a shower off my sister's room. Just don't disturb her mess. Believe me, she'll notice," he says with a laugh. Ricky enters the room and looks around. Posters, books, and DVDs all on topics such as the bizarre, the mystical, and the occult. He has been holding in a piss since chugging down a Gatorade after the game. He quickly tosses his shirt aside, which lands on a stack of books, and he rushes into the bathroom.

He sheds his clothes, hops into the shower, and groans in relief as he pisses in the shower. After a good hot shower, he puts his clothes back on and enters back into Samantha's room. He lifts his tee shirt off the stack of books. He puts on his shirt, which is inside out from when he pulled it off at the basketball court. As he leaves the room, he doesn't take notice of the stack of books that the tee is on. The top book is entitled "Necronomicon," and the second book is "Complete Works of H.P. Lovecraft," and also several Stephen King books.

In the family room, Sean has already powered up his X-Box with his latest first-person shooter (FPS) game. Sean looks up at Ricky and says, "Did you bring another tee shirt? Thought you had that skull tee shirt."

Rickie says, "Nahh… it's just inside-out. Hey, let's play that new shooter game of yours."

Sean is good at the game and slaughters Ricky in quick fashion. So they decide to team up to go after challengers on the web. They find opponents, and before long, the two work well as a team and make it to the next level. After a while, they take a break to get food and drinks. Sean says, "I'm going to get some snacks and brews from the fridge."

As Sean leaves, Ricky stands up and stretches his arms back, and in doing so, the tee shirt comes in contact with his stomach. He feels a tickling sensation on the upper part of his stomach. He immediately touches his stomach with his hand outside the shirt, and the sensation stops. He lifts his hand away, and he feels it again after about 10 seconds. This time, he grabs the shirt and rubs it around. Then pulls it outward to look down between the shirt and skin for anything. Nothing there. He notices the sensation is where the mouth of the skull is. He releases the tee shirt, and within a moment, he feels the nibbling.

He lets it go to time the duration. It nibbles for about 5 seconds and then stops for 3 seconds; nibbles for 7, stops for 4; nibbles 6, stops for 5. Variable. Sean comes back into the room with beers and chips in hand. Ricky goes, "Alright! Thanks for the brew, dude." They kick back and start guzzling beer before resuming the game. Again, the tee shirt is touching his skin, and he feels the nibble. He instinctively pulls up his tee and looks down inside for something… but nothing.

Sean looks over and says, "Are you okay?"

Not wanting him to think he is nuts, Ricky says, "Oh yeah, I think the ink of the skull print is irritating my skin," as he pulls it off, right-sides the tee, and puts it back on. Sean does a slight double take when looking at the skull tee, thinking there is some change to the face. He is quickly distracted when Ricky says, "Who are we gonna play this time?" Sean switches his attention to the screen, and they continue playing.

There is no more incidence with the tee shirt.

When Ricky gets home, he has a bit of a beer buzz going on. He takes off his skull tee shirt, throws it into a pile, and puts on one of his favorites. He feels tired, so he decides to take a nap before dinner. After dinner, he retires to his room to continue binging on that haunted house series. He has about four more episodes to go to finish the first season of 10 episodes. After a couple of episodes, and he is all "spooked-up," he starts thinking about his skull-tee. He starts looking for it in the 'needs-to-be-washed' pile of clothes. When he finds it, he instinctively sniffs the armpits to make sure it isn't too noxious. Then he ponders a moment as he thinks he notices a slight change to the skull face. It is very subtle, but it seems the upward turn of the mouth corners is gone, making the face a little less comical. He shrugs it off. He is curious to see if it still does that nibbling effect, so he turns it inside-out and puts it on.

He doesn't feel anything right away. He lies down and continues to watch the next episode of the show. After a couple of minutes, he feels it. Like the first time it happened, he goes through a series of gestures and tests to confirm the effect.

Comically, he tries to 'catch' the skull nibbling by looking down his shirt and lifting when the sensation starts – quickly, multiple times. But, of course, he never sees anything. He begins to define the logistics of the effect. It only works when the shirt is flush with the skin. It can't be forced by pressing the shirt against the skin, and if he puts his hand there, no nibble. When the shirt is shifted to a different area of the skin, there is no effect. The timing and duration seem to be variable. After a while, he realizes he has been missing his show.

He really feels spooked now, with the shirt and the haunted-house show going on, so he takes off the shirt and throws it in the dirty clothes pile. He notices a red mark on his stomach where the nibbling sensation occurs – it is sensitive to the touch. He puts back on his favorite tee and returns to his show.

The next day after work, Ricky does a load of wash, mostly consisting of his tee shirts. He is particularly interested to see if skull-tee still nibbles after a washing – then he'd be convinced that the white ink - or something on it - was causing the effect. After the wash and dry, he folds up all his tees – it must be 20 or so. He finds the skull-tee and puts it aside. After putting away all the tees, he comes back to try out the skull-tee. When he picks it up to put on, he notices a very subtle change to the skull print – its eyes are a little less happy. Confounded, he gets on his phone to search for a photo of himself wearing the tee shirt from years ago. Whoa. Sure enough, he sees some subtle differences in the skull's appearance. He starts to get spooked out again. He is almost too frightened to put it on, but the curiosity is too intense to deny. He grabs his phone to get a snap of the new look. He then pulls it inside out and puts it on. He waits a few minutes, but nothing. He pats his stomach to possibly 'wake it up,' but still nothing. He begins to think that the washing 'cleared' it out. Eventually, he gets bored and kicks back on the couch to find the next show to binge on. After a few minutes, he feels a little nibble. Moments later, another… and then another, until it's back to its accustomed 'self.' He says to himself, "He's baaaaacccckkkk," in Carol Anne (Poltergeist) fashion.

The next day at the Xchng, Ricky tells Sean about his 'possessed tee shirt.' Of course, Sean doesn't believe him in the least, but Ricky insists, describing when it first happened at Sean's house. Sean says, "So that's why you were acting weird while we were playing the video games."

Ricky explains, "Yeah, that's when it first started happening."

Sean grins and concedes, "I wouldn't doubt if it had something to do with my sister somehow." Ricky says, "As a matter of fact..." before explaining, he's cut off by Sean, who takes quick notice of a good sales opportunity as a group of three coeds enter the store. He says, "Let me check *this* out," and he begins approaching the girls.

Later, while hanging up some new tee shirt arrivals, Ricky is approached by a dejected Sean, who says, "They were just looking." Sean looks at Ricky's skull-tee and asks, "Hey Ricky, how's 'bout I try it on?"

"Sure," says Ricky as he pulls down a tee shirt from the rack, "I'm gonna buy this one to wear 'cause I figured you'd want to wear my 'possessed tee.'"

"*Possessed*...we'll see," Sean says unconvinced. They step into the back room to change shirts.

Ricky pulls the skull-tee inside-out before giving it to Sean and explains, "You have to wear it inside out".

Sean skeptically "Ohhhh kaaay."

Ricky puts on his new one while Sean drapes on the skull-tee. Sean stands for a moment as if expecting something to happen. He gives several gestures to indicate nothing is happening. After a quick shrugging of shoulders, Sean gets a surprised look on his face while looking at Ricky.

Ricky grins and says, "You're feeling it… ain't cha." They both start laughing. Sean does just what Ricky did after each nibble: holds his belly, pats his belly, rubs his belly, looks down in between, and even tries catching it in action by quickly looking in between. Sean goes, "This is so fucking weird!"

Ricky follows, "Yeah, right?"

Sean: "Mind if I wear it for a while?"

Ricky: "Sure… but don't tell anyone else about it, OK?"

Sean: "Yeah, OK… I get it."

For the next 30 minutes, Sean and Ricky work around the store in different areas. Ricky looks at Sean across the store; Sean is already looking back with a nodding grin. Sean later notions to meet in the back. In the backroom, Sean goes, "Duuude!… you got a possessed tee shirt. What are you going to do with it? Have an exorcism?" He laughs, "My sister would've wanted this when she was into that weird shit."

Ricky, with a pensive look, said, "I dunno, I'm gonna lay low with it and see what happens with it."

Wanting to know more about it, Sean asks, "Does it nibble on *any* part of the body?" as he rubs his crotch.

Ricky explains, "I didn't experiment with *every* part of the body, but what I found is 'no'… it only likes the stomach area" in a snarky tone as he stuffs the shirt in his backpack.

Sean, in parting, "Let me know if there's anything else you find, yo bro?"

Ricky replies, "You got it", with a fist-bump departure.

On his way home, he has a satisfied grin on his face that he could validate the skull-tee to his friend. At least it wasn't only in his head. Just when he steps inside the house, it dawns on him, "Ahhhh, shit. I forgot to tell him about the skull face changing." He thinks for a moment, then goes into the living room. He instinctively pulls it out of the bag to see any changes. He pulls out his phone to check the last photo; he zooms in - sure enough, so subtle, maybe a quarter-inch augmentation of the jaws. A little less happy.

He is startled by his folks entering the room. He dare not tell his parents, who are devoutly religious, of any of this story. He knows any mention of a "possessed" *anything* under their roof would absolutely flip them out, and they'd want to get rid of it.

"Honey, isn't that one you used to wear a lot?" his mother asks. "What, are you selling it?"

He makes up some bullshit about the shirt becoming valuable because the artist became famous, and he is now thinking of putting it up for sale.

His dad, smart-alecky, "Whatever. So long as you cover this month's rent."

Ricky gets to his room and spreads out the tee shirt on his bed to take a new photo. He slowly feels the area that has changed, thinking that maybe it would feel different from the other areas of the print. But it doesn't. After much contemplation, he puts the tee aside and leaves the room to go down to have dinner.

It is around 8:30 p.m. when he returns to his room. He puts on his skull-tee inside out. He remembers there is a new show on beginning at 9, but he falls asleep while watching TV. He dozes off and dreams he is doing a talk show where he is describing his possessed tee shirt. While he is describing it to the host, the nibble intensifies to a down-right bite, and the next one is terribly painful. He lifts his shirt to see a horrible, full 3-D skull head, taking a massive chomp out of his stomach. Ricky screams in pain; the head looks up at him and says, "WHAT ARE YOU LOOKING AT?!" … then it lets out a loud belch.

Ricky wakes up in a panic. He instinctively looks down at his stomach to make sure it is all there and then rips off his shirt and flings it to the wall. He lays panting, gasping for breath. He begins to calm down, pats his stomach, and feels relieved it was just a dream.

The next day, on his day off, he is constantly disturbed by the dream. He'll be in the middle of something, and wham, he thinks of it biting him. He decides to get rid of it. He posts an ad on the free online classifieds website: "Possessed T-Shirt."

He posts a photo and explains the logistics of the nibble effect, but he leaves out any mention of falling asleep with it on. He even offers a money-back guarantee if the buyer is not satisfied. He states that the offering is a one-day "Best Offer" and figures if he can get a couple hundred for it, he'd be happy. He also writes in the description, "Great ice-breaker at parties ;-D."

The next day at the Xchng, Sean asks Ricky, "How's 'skull-tee'?"

Ricky goes, "I'm gonna get rid of it."

Super surprised, Sean pleads, "Why??"

Ricky continues, "I found something else about it. You don't fall asleep with it on. It will get into your head and cause a horrible nightmare."

"Well, just don't sleep with it on", Sean suggests.

"No, it's not that simple. I don't even want it around anymore. Now, even awake, I can't get it out of my head," he explains. Ricky tells Sean about the plan to sell it, and Sean offers to help him out with the sale. Sean reads the posting and laughs at the "ice-breaker" and "money-back guarantee offer."

Sean suggests that he dress like a badass for the sale – there's no telling what kind of weirdos might show up. They are all set for next Tuesday when they both have the day off.

Ricky gets numerous calls wanting to know more about it, some out of curiosity, while others claim it to be a hoax. Tuesday comes around, and Sean stops by with a biker gang outfit he put together along with some temporary tattoos – even on his face – to look like someone you wouldn't want to mess with. He plans to just hang out in the background while Ricky does the talking.

The first potential buyer to stop by is a group of four Goths – two guys and two gals. Despite the head Goth trying it on and admitting that it is nibbling, he says, "It's not scary enough." They leave without an offer but call back in 10 minutes to offer $40 for it.

The next are a couple of nerdy, geek guys. They each try it on, and one feels it, but the other does not. They dismiss the possession by suggesting that Ricky put some irritant on the teeth of the skull to get the effect. Ricky explains that if you move the skull print to the side, there is no effect. But they are not convinced and leave with no offer.

The next buyer comes by himself and introduces himself as Damien. He has a creepy aura about him, and Sean makes his presence more apparent by standing next to Ricky during the interaction. Damien does what seems to be the ritual: puts it on, is surprised by the initial nibble, rubbing stomach, looks down in between, allows it to nibble a few times, and then tries to catch it in action. He ends up saying, "It doesn't bite hard enough," which causes Ricky and Sean to exchange odd glances. But then he asks what the high bid is.

Ricky, in an effort to get rid of the eerie guy, says $200. Sean looks at Ricky, but then, surprisingly, the buyer contemplates for a moment and says, "I'll give you $250 for it." Ricky nonchalantly says, "OK, let me get your name and number, and if you're the high bidder, we'll give you a call." After 'Damien leaves, Ricky and Sean look at each other and laugh with high-fives.

Sean goes, "$250! Bro, I think you got something here!"

The next buyer is a group of 3 women who immediately describe their new-age outlook on life. With our guy's backs turned, the first two try it on and giggle uncontrollably with the effect. The third woman, younger with a buxom figure, puts it on, but her boobs are so big the shirt is not able to make contact with the skin. Her two friends have to pull the shirt back from the sides to make contact in the stomach area. She begins giggling, and Ricky and Sean stare wantonly at the bosomy sight with dopy grins on their faces. The women say they are interested but balk at the high bid so far, and they say they'll think about it.

Before the next buyer shows up, a few more calls come in. Some express interest, while others are turned off by the high bid.

Fifteen minutes later, the next potential buyers come in. Ricky and Sean are shocked to greet a priest and a nun at the door. He's about 60, whereas she is in her mid-30s. They cordially introduce themselves and proceed to the family room. The Father says to the Sister, "Are you ready for this?" She nods obediently. The Father asks Ricky, "Do you have someplace she can try it on?" He says, "Oh yeah, the bathroom." Moments later, the three males are standing in the hallway outside the bathroom door, each with arms folded, glancing at one another – Ricky and Sean are trying not to laugh. Finally, she says behind the door, "Oh Father… Father, it tickles!" and starts tittering. The Father sternly said, "Now Sister, remember what I told you. What you need to ask yourself: 'Is this a tool of the devil?'" Confidently she says, "Yes… yes, I believe it is." He says, "OK, get dressed and come out here ASAP." The Father looks at Ricky. "You say the bid is at $250? Ok, we'll make it $300. Excuse me while I make a call to the diocese," as he leaves for the family room. The bathroom door opens, and she steps out dressed in her nun's outfit and hands Ricky the skull-tee. Ricky glances into the bathroom and asks the Sister, "Is that yours?" pointing at the bra hanging over the shower curtain. She blushingly shouts, "Oh my!" as she instinctively covers her bosom and quickly goes back in. When they finally leave, Ricky and Sean are grinning at each other, Sean going, "Dude, you can't *buy* this kind of entertainment!"

Next are three neo-Nazis. Like the goths, they complain it's not scary enough. Besides, they were hoping it talked, also. Hearing the high bid, they, too, say they'll think about it, but not without one of them giving Sean the stink-eye when they leave. He whispers to Sean, "Where did you get that outfit, the Xchng?"

Next comes the paranormal researchers. Two guys from the local university who study the paranormal and do side gigs for money and kicks. Ricky quips, "So, are you like Ghostbusters?" One looks at the other and says, "Yeah, you could say something like that." After trying it out, they say they like it but have to confer with one another. They excuse themselves momentarily to make a call. They come back to Ricky and say "OK, how about $350?" Ricky responds, "Sure. We're taking bids all day long. If you're the highest, we'll contact you. The bidding will end at 9 o'clock sharp."

By 8 pm, they've seen a dozen potential buyers with the high bid at $550 from a sexy couple in their 40s that were enticed by the 'ice-breaker' claim. They said they want it for the swinger parties they host. They wanted to go into graphic descriptions about their parties, but Ricky kept it to business. About five people called back asking about the highest bid so far and seemed very interested. Ricky tells them there will be a final auction that will start at 9 p.m. Ricky and Sean move their operation to the garage and open the garage door to prepare for the final bidders.

At 8:45, the garage has about 12 bidders still interested, including the priest and nun, the goths, the swingers, and the paranormal guys. By 8:59, the bidding had climbed to $800 from the paranormal guys. The clock hits

9, and just when Ricky says, "Going once… going twice…" a voice from the back says, ", Twelve hundred."

The paranormal guys shrink while everyone goes silent and looks toward the back. Standing outside the garage is Damien, who had the money all along but waited till the last second to make the big bid. Wide-eyed and grinning, Ricky says, "Going once… going twice… SOLD to the man in the back for twelve hundred!"

Damien steps up and hands Ricky 12 one-hundred dollar bills, who gratefully receives the skull-tee from Sean and heads toward his late model Corvette. Ricky runs over to him and, before Damien gets into his car, says to him, "Just one other thing… *don't fall asleep with it on.* You just might have a horrible nightmare."

But rather than being frightened, Damien says, "I like that! Anything else?"

Ricky: "Oh yeah, keep taking photos of the skull face. I swear it's changing."

Damien says, "I'm liking this more and more," as he reaches into his pocket and hands Ricky another $200, adding, "Text me the photos you've taken so far." He proceeds to hop into the Vette, and just before he leaves, he rolls down the window and asks Ricky, "You can wash it, right?"

"Yeah, didn't affect it," says Ricky as Damien nods and speeds away. Ricky returns to the garage as all the other bidders are still standing stunned.

When Ricky gets back to Sean, he hands him $200 and says, "Thanks for helping out with this, bro."

Sean, with a huge grin, "Anytime! Let me know when you get *another* possessed t-shirt!"

Afterward, Ricky's folks asked him what was going on in the garage. He explains that the tee shirt turned out to be *very* valuable and that he had an auction for it. He's totally relieved that they never found out about its possession.

His dad sarcastically said, "Great timing; your rent is due today."

BYRON

Turns out Damien's real name is Byron, who owns a curio shop with many exotic, bizarre, and occult items in the Santa Monica area. He has always liked the name Damien and lives out an alter ego when using it. The first thing he does is lay out his newfound prize and take several good photos of it. He is fascinated by wearing the skull-tee and feeling the nibbling sensation. Eventually, he puts skull-tee in a display case behind the counter of his store, where he takes several more photos of it. He has placed a $10,000 price tag on it and will allow only serious buyers to try it on.

That evening, he decides to sleep with it on and take on the dream challenge that Ricky forewarned. He lounges on a sofa watching a documentary on paranormal activity investigation, all the time enjoying the nibbling from his new friend. He becomes curious if the skull would nibble on his groin to get sexual gratification. He pulls down his pants and takes off his shirt so it is still inside out but with the skull print coming in contact with his junk. After a moment, he starts feeling it, grinning more and more. Then, it starts getting more painful. Until finally, a huge bite is taken - removing his lower appendage. He screams and looks down to see a 3-D head of a hideous skull look up at him and say, "WHAT ARE YOU LOOKING AT? … BUUURRRP!"

He wakes up in a panic. He instinctively checks his junk to make sure it's still there. *Thank God!* He quickly pulls off the shirt and throws it across the room. "Oh gawd, thank the lord, it was only a dream." He lays back, breathing heavily for a while.

After a rough night's sleep, he gets up, collects the shirt, and spreads it out to reposition it in the display case. He notices a change to the appearance of the skull – a subtle shift to the brow to make it a little angrier. He gets his camera to capture the change. He compares the image to the images received from Ricky. All during the course of the day, he is haunted by his nightmare the night before, cringing every time it enters his thoughts. His mind is focused on marketing it now and to get it out of his possession. Later that day, he starts making calls to known clients who he feels would be interested in it, as well as several other curio shop owners in his network across the nation. As the shirt remains in the case, he gets a call from a fellow shop owner in the LA area with an eccentric, celebrity clientele. Xavier has someone in mind who may be very interested in the shirt, and he is willing to introduce his client to Byron, provided a finder's fee is established. The two make an appointment to bring the client over to see it, but only under the strictest and most discreet arrangements to keep his client's identity a secret.

The appointment time comes near. Byron makes sure the shop is clear of any other customers, and he flips the OPEN sign to CLOSED. Moments later, a black limo pulls up in front of the shop. Xavier first comes to the door and makes sure the coast is clear. Once confirmed, he nods to the limo, and a big bodyguard gets out to escort a cloaked figure who is pinching closed the hood of the jacket. Judging by the feet, the figure appears to be a female. Once all are inside, Byron locks the door and pulls down the shades. The four are now in front of the counter looking at the skull tee in the display case, now fitted with a series of progressive photos showing the facial changes to the skull print. A faint chuckle is heard from the cloaked figure. Byron proceeds to reiterate the logistics of the possession while laying out the photos of the progressive morphing of the skull face. Byron allows the cloaked person to try it on in the back room, escorted by the bodyguard. While still in the front store area by the counter, Byron and Xavier hear a tittering laugh from the buyer – sounding like an elderly woman. After a few minutes, the cloaked figure and bodyguard reemerge from the backroom. The bodyguard nods and hands Byron a prepared money order for the $10K.

Happy but slightly surprised, Byron offers, "Would you like the display case for the shirt, Madame?" The cloaked figure nods, and the bodyguard assists in taking it out to the limo. Following the others out, Xavier turns toward Byron and says with a grin and pumping fist, "Alright. I'll give you a couple of days to cash it, and I'll stop by for my finder's fee. Good going, Byron."

Byron: "No, thank *you*."

VIVIAN

Once back in her Bel Air estate, Vivian removes her cloak and undresses to experience her new delight. Bruno, who is also her butler, brings in the display case. Vivian is one of those aging stars from the tail-end of Hollywood's 'Golden Age,' and she hasn't been in a movie in decades. She had played leading lady roles for the likes of Warren Beatty, Burt Reynolds, and Paul Neumann. Now in her 80s, she has shunned the 'old lady' roles offered to her and prefers to have people remember her for her beauty when in her 30s.

She became interested in metaphysics when in her 50s to find a remedy for fighting the aging process. She even dabbled in the black arts for a quick fix and possible reversal of aging. She bought the shirt believing that this may be a possible portal to reaching a deal with the devil for immortality.

Knowing that it will cause a nightmare, she purposefully wears it and retires in her room with the hopes of meeting Lucifer, Beelzebub, and Mephistopheles - whatever the name – so long as she can make a deal.

An hour later, Bruno hears a bloodcurdling scream from her room and rushes to her aid. She is non-responsive, and he calls 911 and then begins administering CPR. When paramedics come, they want to cut off the shirt, but Bruno yells, "No!" and he proceeds to slip it off her before paramedics continue. "It's one of her favorites," says Bruno, as the paramedics give one another odd looks.

Lying in a hospital bed, Vivian grabs Bruno's hand and angrily says, "Bruno, I want you to get rid of that, that *abomination*! I don't want it in my house when I get home from here, do you understand? Contact Xavier to sell it for me as soon as possible. I want a million bucks for it."

Bruno nods obediently, "Yes, my love."

Xavier begins making calls and encourages his contacts to spread the word in celebrity circles about a possessed tee shirt. He stops by Byron's curio to pick up his finder's fee for $1500. He says to Byron, "Yeah, the old bag is selling it already… her bum-ticker nearly exploded when she fell asleep with it on."

Byron, shaking his head, "I forewarned her. Looks like you might be up for another commission if you sell it for her, X-man".

Xavier: "Yeah bro, and it'll be a lot more! She wants a million bucks for it."

"What the fuck?! Yer shitting me, eh?"

"For real, dude."

As Xavier is laying out the t-shirt to display in a newer, more impressive showcase with the progressive photos lining the bottom of the case, he notices the differences between the last photo taken and the skull's current look. More angrier… and now with two small bumps on either side of the forehead - could those be sprouting horns? Later, he is adding a new photo print to the line-up – now totaling six.

D'EMILIO

Word gets to the likes of D'emilio Sands (AKA D'e), a super-rich, highly successful fighter with money to burn. After tiring of collecting the most expensive exotic sports cars, he began collecting bizarre artifacts - things you'd expect to see in the Smithsonian. When he is entertaining a new, influential friend, he likes to show off and impress with his collection.

One of D'emilio's minions is assigned to go to Xavier's curio shop and try on the t-shirt. If he feels the nibble, he is to contact D'emilio. Soon, the 400-pound minion is at Xavier's, has the skin-tight tee on, and is giggling uncontrollably while on the phone with D'e. "It tickles, boss… (he straightens up) …but yeah, it's the real deal." Soon, a brigade of 3 hot-wheel Hummers pulls up to Xavier's shop.

Later, at his mansion pad, D'emilio is chillin' with his posse. They're partying big-time to celebrate the purchase with the champagne flowing along with other party favors - catering to please. The skull-tee is on display prominently in a special 5' x 8' room he has made, just off the party room.

Later that evening, when everyone is drunk, high, or passed out, D'e decides to prank one of his minions. He taps the shoulder of Deangelo and says, "Hey, let's prank Reggie." D'e goes and gets the tee shirt. They shake Reggie from his stupor and tell him, "Hey buddy, it's your turn to try it! Yeah, you'll have some incredible visions!"

Reggie sloppily puts the shirt on and lays back. He drunkenly chuckles at the nibbling sensation and before long dozes off with a stupid grin on his face. D'e and Deangelo are grinning and barely able to keep their own eyes open when Reggie starts frowning and gasping for air. The big, muscular minion screams like a little girl. Reggie starts grabbing and practically tears at the shirt to get it off. D'e shouts, "Get it off him!" fearing he'll ruin the shirt.

D'e is carefully putting his prize back in the display case. In the party room, the show 'Fact or Fraud?' is on the TV - a weekly show that challenges and tests supposedly paranormal objects and guests. The show is hosted by that shock-comic Raphael Rivera. D'e checks the photos from the hi-res image sent by Xavier against the 'new' face. "Well, I'll be damned." Again, the eye sockets have molded to a more angry appearance. He looks toward the TV in the other room with the show still on. D'emilio figures if he can get the skull-tee on the show, the value of it would soar. He arranges a meeting with the producers of the show.

In an exchange that could be interpreted as antagonist, the two parties eventually agree to terms – go figure. They write up a contract that specifies payment and what will be done with the item on the show. They agree that skull-tee will appear on next week's show.

RAPHAEL

The Night of the show that will feature D'emilio's skull-tee rolls around. In his usual bombastic flair, Raphael Rivera (RR) jokes and demeans all of the objects that are given to him. Paranormal objects that move on their own; a possessed hat; a phone that receives calls from the dead; a cat that says, "I'm gonna kill you" when it is annoyed; and more.

Next comes skull-tee. A nerdy assistant to RR brings out the shirt on a hanger. RR starts, "Oh, and what do we have here? So I'm told this is a possessed tee shirt. They say the skull will *nibble,* yes, NIBBLE on your stomach when worn inside out. It is owned by a VERY well-known celebrity in the Malibu area, and he let us use this tonight. I'm going to try it on," as the audience cheers him on. D'e is outraged because he wants them to say his name. It was in the contract – his ego was expecting it. He gets on the phone and dials his attorney while still watching the show.

In the meantime, Raphael is putting on the inside-out tee shirt and having a snarky, fun time with it. He goes through the usual routine when someone puts it on for the first time, but he exaggerates his responses for laughs. RR points to his stomach. "They say it only nibbles here, but I say 'why stop there?'… how about here?" as he lowers the tee to his groin area. Everybody is laughing, even D'e's minions.

D'e freezes while watching the TV and mutters to himself, "He wasn't supposed to do that."

Then, in his typical over-the-top way, RR yells out, "What if I kiss it?" The audience roars. He puts it over his head and mimics a French kiss with the inside-out tee shirt over his head.

Suddenly, the shirt bulges large and comes down on Raphael's head with a huge CHOMP sound. The tee shirt collapses onto his headless shoulders. For a slight moment, you could hear a pin drop, but then about a fifth of the audience started clapping and laughing, thinking it was one of his gags. Then Raphael's knees buckle, and he goes down kneeing – blood streaming down his white dress shirt.

The cheering diminishes. A shocked D'e drops the phone and approaches the TV while a couple of the minions are laughing, still thinking it's a gag.

Raphael's nerdy assistant snaps out of his shock, turns to the audience, and says, "OK… let's all just be calm." At that moment, the entire audience panics and rush for the doors. The studio is cleared within 15 seconds of the audience, leaving only the stage crew. Finally, somebody hollers, "Somebody call 911!"

Back at D'emilio's, one of his minions stupidly says, "Hey boss, it should be worth tons more now!"

D'e snaps back, "You idiot, I'll be lucky to get it back now!"

Ricky and Sean are watching together at Sean's parents, both slack-jawed with bulging eyes. In unison, they shout, "Are you fucking kidding me!?"

Byron, lounging on his sofa watching, "Jeez, sure glad *I* didn't try kissing it."

Vivian, alone in her hospital bed, laughs hysterically and says, "I never liked that Rivera guy! Serves him right!"

When the local police get there, the body is still hunched over and on his knees in a puddle of blood. The homicide detective's first question is "How did he lose his head?" They all go into the production control room, where they roll back the video and show him.

When the FBI agents Holder and Sully get there, the male immediately says, "OK… we're taking over from here," while holding up his credentials. After oddly looking at the corpse, his first question is, "How did he lose his head?"

D'e makes his way into the studio, demanding his tee shirt back. Holder explains, "Sorry, Mr. Johnson, it is crime scene evidence now."

Jackson goes, "WHAT?! (Long rant) …Anyways, it's JACKSON… *Mister* JACKSON to YOU."

Holder calmly, "Well, Mr. Jackson, you may actually be responsible… that is, liable for the death of Mr. Rivera, seeing how this is YOUR property. Therefore I would not expect to get possession of the shirt any time soon if I were you. Haha, I made a joke. Possession… get it?"

Jackson stomps away with a tantrum and starts dialing his lawyer. In all seriousness, he asks, "Saul, can… can they arrest me if my shirt kills someone?" After a pause, he says excitedly, "I'm not kidding! Did you watch the Fact or Fraud show tonight?!"

On the other end of the line, Saul is prone on the carpet in only his boxer shorts while two hookers are doing coke on his mountainous belly.

FBI

The FBI agents take the t-shirt and all other evidence to a small room in the basement of the FBI building with the homemade sign 'Z-FILES' posted on the door. Their first test involves scraping some of the skull-print ink for analysis. The chemical breakdown indicates that it is a standard, white plastisol ink – nothing unusual about that.

Next, they do a study with a fixed camera on it for hours… On a table, the shirt is propped up, inside-out, with a fixed camera on the inside focused on the skull print. The table is in an isolated exam room with a window that is observed from a control room. A goofy, nerdy monitor guy, no doubt a low-level rookie agent, is assigned to watch the recording video to report anything. After seeming interested for the first couple of hours, he gets bored and starts playing on his phone for hours. After about 6 hours, he's snoring soundly. A sensor alarm goes off to indicate some visual alteration has occurred, and it wakes him up… He sees the white ink of the skull slowly sink away into the blackness of the tee shirt. Suddenly, a hideous, monstrous skull comes full 3-D towards the camera and chomps. The guy yelps and lunges backward as he and the chair fall back onto the floor. The video now records only static snow.

Ricky's parents are watching a news clip about the broadcasted decapitation of Rivera. His mom says from the other room, "Ricky honey, isn't that the shirt you auctioned a few weeks ago?"

While he's thinking of something to say, his dad goes, "Ohhhh… BTW… your rent is due today."

Behind a closed door with the title CIA Deputy Director Marshall McKlun, two men are watching the FBI video of the t-shirt. Along with McKlun is General Halftrack. After watching the video, the General looks at McKlun and says, "Yeah, I think I can use that." McKlun responds, "Very well. Let me make a few calls, and I'll get that into your hands."

CIA

A couple of CIA agents show up at the Z-FILES office to claim the t-shirt. When they arrive, they find Holder observing a small pig in restraints with the shirt in contact with its belly. Holder is sitting with his chin in his hand, waiting for the pig to fall asleep. The CIA agents explain they are 'appropriating' the shirt for undisclosed operations but hint that they are going to 'test' it more.

In a clandestine rendezvous, McKlun hands over to General Halftrack a steel attaché case.

The military immediately started using it to intimidate terrorist prisoners. They force them to watch the "Fact or Fraud" show and the FBI video. Afterward, when the interrogator threatens to cover the head of the terrorist with the shirt, they break down crying and start singing like canaries. For weeks, it proved to be a most effective device to elicit confessions and information from terrorists. Well, that is, until Abul Hasan Al-Zziz.

When he is brought in for interrogation, Al-Zziz is viciously spewing vile insults and taunting in his native language to anyone who will look at him. Even without knowing his language, one can tell he is taunting and mocking his captors to 'go-head and put it on my head.' They strap him down face-up on a plank. Never having to go this far, the torturer brings over the shirt to put over his head. Bob, the torturer, holds up the t-shirt for Al-Zziz to see, then pulls it inside out. He proceeds to place it over Al-Zziz's head, who is laughing insanely and spewing more taunting insults. With the shirt over his head, he even starts imitating kissing the shirt, as Rivera did. But nothing happens. They wait for about 30 seconds, but nothing happens all along, Al-Zziz continuing his insane laughing. They all look at one another dumbfounded and then into the CCTV camera.

One of the two interrogators decides to take it off Al-Zziz and, for some unknown reason, tests it on himself. Suddenly, the shirt bulges large, and a huge chomp is heard. The other interrogator is horrified and looks into the CCTV camera with a confused, terrified look. In the monitoring room, the colonel stares at the monitor and shouts, "What the HELL just happened?"

Monitoring the video is Pvt. Dufus: "I think the shirt just chomped off his head."

The General vehemently turns to Dufus, "I CAN SEE THAT! WHY? Why didn't it work on that frickin' psycho Al-Zziz?!"

The next day, the colonel and two of his lead interrogators are standing in front of General Halftrack's desk. Halftrack sarcastically "*So…* Now we *know…* you have to put it on *yourself…* DIDN'T ANYBODY THINK TO TEST THAT?!" The colonel & men look sheepish, as if guilty dogs. The General continues, "Do you think any of those assholes terrorists will put it on *themselves*? Especially after that *Psycho* Al-Zziz spreads the word. (long pause) So what do *YOU* want to tell that young man's… ah, Bob's folks?"

(McKlun's Dream) Countless hands are grasping at the skull-tee as it gently floats up into the air, where an eagle swoops down and flies into the shirt and is now wearing it. The bird flies around, landing on people's heads and decapitating them. After several decapitations, an alarm is heard, getting louder and louder. Suddenly, McKlun wakes up and answers the ringing phone. After catching his breath, he says, "Tell the General to meet me in my office at 10 this morning." He looks at the clock; it is 4:04 in the morning.

CIA Director Marshal McKlun meets with General Halftrack. "Well… it looks like our little *secret weapon* is useless now. I don't know what you want to do with it from this point on," says Halftrack as he tosses the shirt onto McKlun's desk.

McKlun picks up the shirt and holds it up to look at the skull, now sporting horns… and canine teeth. He says, "I'll take it from here, General, thank you." After the general leaves, he gets on the phone, dials, and waits for the caller to answer. He simply says, "Yes, I've got it." Listens for a moment, "How soon can you gather the group?"

Later that evening, McKlun is at home looking at the skull-tee hanging on a hanger. He has all the photos in front of him as he compares the latest changes. After contemplating for a while, he unbuttons his pajama top and stands topless. He approaches the skull-tee and considers putting it on. As he begins reaching for the shirt, it flutters, and a loud belch sound is heard.

He backs off in shock. Once he re-composes himself, he takes the shirt and locks it in another room.

THE FOUR

On a night of heavy rain, several luxury cars pull up to a countryside mansion. From each, a chauffeur escorts with umbrellas, their important passengers to the door.

As each of the elderly men comes in through the massive front double doors, a butler obediently gathers their coats and canes. A priest, a rabbi, and an imam, each in ceremonial garb are received. McKlun greets them all in while wearing his own ceremonial-ritual garment - an eclectic combination of many religious and spiritual beliefs.

They gather at a round table in the large study with lots of books – covering all four walls. It is a meticulously organized room with many ancient artifacts on display. In the middle of the table is a large, 3-foot wide metal bowl with a cross of wood standing up in the middle of the bowl. On that cross is a tee shirt. The shirt displays a wickedly hideous horned skull, almost dragon-like head.

McKlun walks around and hands each member a 3-foot stick with a flame at the end. Once seated, he begins to say, "All-encompassing God – God of all nations, all creeds. Free us of this abomination and blasphemy to all that is good of nature and of the dignity of humankind." They all hold their flames under the tee shirt. He continues, "Free us from this indignity and rid us of this unholy and cursed object of the devil with the purifying fire which we bestow." They begin chanting in Latin verse but start to become perplexed because, despite being dosed with a flammable fluid, skull-tee does not ignite.

Suddenly, the tee bursts with green flames and becomes engulfed in a fireball, illuminating the room with a putrid green glow. The four men are horrified and cast their stick flames haphazardly. The center fireball bursts outward in four directions, turning into arcs, then into necks with hydra heads. They all scream in terror. The hydra heads chomp down on the head of each man, decapitating them all. The housekeepers are frantically trying to enter the room to assist, but the doors are locked.

The four headless corpses still sit upright at the table while the room becomes engulfed in red & yellow flames.

The next day, fire investigators are sifting through the rubble for clues. The FBI investigator, looking at the four charred bodies, confoundedly asks "Where the hell are their heads?" They determine the origin of the fire to be that of a metal canister of gasoline next to one wall of books. Next to the canister is a burned stick with a wick. In the metal bowl on the table is just ash. They have been able to identify the four men, but everything else is a mystery. What were they doing? And why?

***

Days later, and after several rainstorms, the rubble has turned to sludge. Local clean-up services are employed to clean the area for final clearance and eventual demolition of this part of the mansion.

One of the work crew, a young 20-something doing 60 days of community service, is shoveling sludgy debris into a wheel barrel. He notices some dark rag or piece of clothing that he is about to dump. He pulls it off the shovel and discovers it is a tee shirt. He douses it with water from his water bottle and wipes off most of the sludge. He notices the print of a skull head. It has the face of a simple, comical, slightly grinning skull. He likes it and wrings out the tee shirt as much as he can, stuffs it in his coat pocket, and continues his cleanup.

THE END

Danny's Thing

A Lesson in Panspermia

Bruce Clark Bennett - ©2023

60 Million Years Ago

In a nearby solar system, two building-sized asteroids are on a collision course. One was somewhat spherical; the other was oblong, almost cigar-shaped, and spinning at an oblique axis. Their angle of incidence was about 120 degrees when they crashed… well, more like a fender-bender. The monolithic behemoths side-swiped one another with tons and tons of debris littering the site as each began new trajectories. Millions of shards of carbonate and ice are left in the wake.

* * *

In the Near Future

Danny is having the thrill of a lifetime, for at least within his young 10 years. His dad, Toby (Albright), is taking him to a meeting with his old high school friend Justin while the two are in Justin's hometown. Justin works at the observatory for astrophysics at the top of the mountain on the big island. As with many youngsters his age, Danny caught the fascination bug for space and astronomy. He had been to a planetarium before, but this was his first opportunity to go to an actual observatory, and he was giddy with anticipation.

It was dusk, and you could already see a plethora of stars in the sky. On the trek up the steep climb to the mountain-top facility in the rental SUV, his dad says to Danny. "Justin and I go way back as high school buddies. We were 'best buds' until we each went off to different colleges, different careers, different lives," as he has a moment of introspection. "If you are polite and well-behaved, Justin might let you see the new interactive telescope they are beta testing."

They knock on the secure doors of the facility and are greeted by Justin. Toby and Justin make long-awaited hellos, starting with a 3-step handshake, a hug, and then start with immediate small talk. Toby: "Look at you! Justin Joiner, the big Doctor of Astrophysics!" Justin: "You haven't done too badly for yourself! Your business is doing great. You took the financial path, whereas I took the science path."

Justin gives Toby and Danny a quick tour around the facility, showing the large telescope and control room.

"And here's the new baby," as they enter the room with the makeshift sign 'Gyro' and approach the geodesic spherical device, about 2.5 meters across.

Toby asks, "Gyro?" Justin: "Short for gyroscope - It's easier than calling it the '360-degree, fully immersible, interactive, quantum telescope'."

Justin opens the hatch and climbs into the cockpit of the snug device while Toby and Danny stick their heads through the portal.

Justin proceeds to show how the Gyro works.

"It is wired-in to all the major feeds available around the world, including the James Webb and new Hubble 3 orbiting telescope."

After a while, Justin says, "Toby, let's go to the breakroom and get that beer I promised you, and we'll catch up on details." He looks at Danny, "You ready to try it?" Danny wide-eyed: "Are you kidding?!"

Justin climbs out, and Danny excitedly climbs into the cockpit. Justin shows him just enough to get him started, and before parting, he says, "Kid, you're going to see things nobody has ever seen before. Enjoy." After looking at Toby, he winks and says to Danny, "Who knows, maybe you'll discover a new star, and we can name it after you." Danny excitedly said, "I could go for that!" They all laugh. Before they leave, Toby says to his son, "Remember, it's not a *toy*."

"Toby, let's get that beer, and I'll tell you what's been happening." As they're walking away, "Tell me, whatever happened to that hot Marilyn Ackerman you took to the prom? Everybody thought you two were going to get married." Their voices become indistinct as Danny begins playing on the device.

Toby and Justin are in the breakroom having a couple of suds while Danny continues to be awe-struck by the 360-degree, interactive telescope. He begins by calling out each planet in the solar system. The telescope rotates the projection and brings the spoken planet front and center. Danny alternates between voice commands to increase the zoom and using his hands to 'manually' do the zoom. He is enthralled by the details of the planets.

After about 45 minutes and several beers later, Toby says to Justin, "Well, great catching up with you. We should let you get back to your work. I need to go take a whiz. I'll meet you back at the 'Gyro.' You may want to make sure Danny hasn't *broken* it yet" with a grin.

Just at that time, Danny is looking perplexed at a strange phenomenon. He is zoomed-in on a grainy 60x60 pixel white blip, but there appear to be black specks moving about over the star – as if "bugs" were crawling across the star. The specks would appear, maybe move, get bigger or smaller, and then disappear.

Just then, that main portion of the screen goes black, startling Danny. He sits there for a while, heart racing and a sick feeling like he has just broken this new, expensive device.

Justin pops in to check on Danny, "Hey, little guy, you bored with it yet, Danny?"

Danny nearly jumps out of the seat. Shocked and nearly panicking: "I… I think I broke it, Dr. Justin, sir."

Justin calmly: "No, no, I'm sure you didn't break it… What do you mean, what happened?"

Danny: "Well, I had this rather odd-looking star in focus, but then everything went black. I didn't break it, did I?"

Justin: "No, probably what happened was the array you were tapped into changed direction or just went off-line. That can happen sometimes. Doesn't occur very often, but I forgot to tell you that could happen. Nothing to worry about."

Danny, with much relief, "Thank God! I thought I broke it or something."

Just then, Toby joins in jokingly: "He broke it, didn't he?"

Justin, tongue in cheek, "Yeah, he did. It's gonna take a couple million dollars to fix!"

At first, Toby's heart skips a beat but quickly calms as he knows he is just joking. Kidding that goes back to their high school days. Danny nervously chuckles.

With Danny still seated, Justin reaches in and double-taps his finger to open a menu that has a history log. "Looks like you were focused on Alpha Centauri C."

Danny assures, "Yeah, that's right! That's what I was looking at."

Justin issues a voice command: "Gyro, Reset all." The total, complete star map resets to the current positioning. "Gyro, Focus: Alpha Centauri" as the map rotates and the star comes front and center to Danny on the 360-screen.

Justin commands: "Gyro, Switch to Hubble 3." Justin glances at the two and says, "This will take a minute or two as the H3 has to position. (pauses, looks at Danny) So Danny, how would you describe this anomaly?"

Danny says, "Well, it looked like tiny specks were crawling across the star. Sorta like bugs."

Justin asks, "Danny, do you mind if I take control of Gyro?"

Just then, as the two are switching positions, an alert pops up to indicate an H3 connection. "Well, alright, let's see what we can see. Gyro, repeat focus of 9:33 pm tonight." As Gyro repositions, it starts zooming in.

Danny explains, "I was looking at one of the exoplanets of Alpha Centauri system; it has six planets that we know of."

Justin: "Very good. Few people would know that."

For the next 20 minutes, they looked at all six exoplanets of Alpha Centauri, but none looked as Danny described.

Toby says, "Yo, Justin, we don't want to put you out like this. We can get going and let you get back to your regular work."

Justin: "Hey, no worries. This is what I normally do. Hey wait…. Wha…? (frowns and focuses) What is this?" as he manually zooms into a very dim point in the constellation.

Danny excitedly said, "Hey, that's it! That's what I was talking about… and it looks a little clearer now."

Justin mutters, "Well, I'll be damned. This was never picked up before. But now, with the enhanced magnification, we can see it." He looks at Danny with a grin, "See? I told ya, little dude. You'd see things nobody has seen before!"

Justin opens a menu of Filters to adjust the display of the image.

Danny jokingly, "Wow, I didn't know about *those* controls."

After a while, Justin turns to Danny and says, "Young man, I think you're on to something big here. Start thinking of what you wanna call it," with a chuckle.

Within a few days, Justin released his findings to the science community. The news gets to the mainstream media. Back in Danny's hometown in Ohio, a local TV reporter interviews Danny.

Danny says, "I'm calling it 'Danny's Thing'." The internet is abuzz with memes and makes international news.

Danny is proud of his discovery, and many congratulate him. However, older kids are jealous and tease him, "Hey Danny, what's yer 'thing'? Is it yer dick? Hahaha".

As astronomers and laypeople clamor to view and comment, speculations range from some sort of small dwarf with sun-spot activity to swarming living creatures.

Countries are excited about the news, and a new space race develops as the United States, Russia, China, and Japan all begin plans to develop a probe to study the mysterious phenomenon. Despite several countries already planning on Mars projects and studies for colonization, the golden fleece of extraterrestrial life lures every nation to be the first to get there. The competition led to the development of advanced solar sail applications to expedite the 4.3 light-year journey. Eventually, nations realize they will achieve better and quicker results if they all work together; a global space task force is formed to coordinate and assemble the multinational efforts and technologies to unify the collective energies. The Exo-Planetary Commission (EPC) was born. Nearly every nation participates to some degree, but of course, the US, Russia, China, Japan, and England played the biggest roles. They are known as the Principal Five.

Once establishing realistic timelines for the technological developments necessary, the EPC sets a goal of 12 years to fully develop and lift off on a manned mission to Alpha Centauri.

The small red dwarf star is designated and officially named Proxima Centauri Beta, about the size of Jupiter. Due to its small size, it was undetected until the Hubble 3 was commissioned and, of course, Danny's discovery.

Incredible scientific strides are made by participating nations, most notably in the field of cryogenic hibernation and solar sail technology. Many of the once-theoretical notions of cryo-sleep/hibernation were now coming to fruition. This technology has become one of the most sought-after holy grails. Venture capitalists pour money into start-ups with promising test results, which further fuels R&D.

Despite gallant efforts and millions in seed money, the technology of gravitational simulation/

stabilization in zero-G proved to remain elusive. The notion of centrifugal forces on the spaceship proved cost-prohibitive and impractical. Instead, the technology of magnetic flooring with specialized body suits proved to be the viable and practical way to go. Innovative methods of mass detection and velocity sensitivity in the magnetic flooring helped actualize and simulate realistic one-g forces.

After several years, quibbling and disagreements forced Russia and China to pull out of the EPC to develop their own combined program to send a manned mission to Alpha Centauri – with a planned lift-off date sooner than the EPC. The Russo-Chino-Space Program (RCSP) was born. France and India take up the fourth and fifth spots in the EPC.

Over the next several years, the EPC begins planning for the crew, establishing rigorous testing for applicants for the Alpha Centauri Mission. The nationality of crew members is based on the financial contributions of each country. Due to the United States' overwhelming financial commitment to the program, they are awarded two positions on the crew. Justin has secured the first spot, as he has early on been a major proponent of the project.

Eight Years Later

The Russo-Chino-Space Program (RCSP) gets ready for lift-off, a full two years ahead of the original plan of the EPC. The RCSP crew consists of three Russians and three Chinese – two males and one female for each nation. As would be expected, the RCSP shares little with the rest of the world – but of course, garner anything they can from the ECP and other research gone public.

In the meantime, Danny is currently getting his Ph.D. in Astrophysics, with a minor in Astrobiology from Caltech. He had some difficult years with all the fame and attention brought on to his younger years because of the discovery at age 10. His early teen years were wrought with drug use and mischievous behavior – leading to some trouble with the law. Contributing was his father's failed business during the recession – losing his business, his wife, and eventually his life. Danny was scared straight during his high school days when his dad's old friend Justin intervened and gave Danny direction and purpose – specifically, the possibility of participation in the mission to Alpha Centauri.

Unbeknownst to the RCSP, scientific contributions from Japan and France have developed a more advanced Solar-Sail technology, which should shave four to five years off the travel time to Alpha Centauri.

Justin and Danny have a heart-to-heart discussion over a drink. Justin assures Danny he will not receive any favoritism during the selection process for the mission crew just because he is the discoverer – he has got to earn it, just like everyone else. Justin: "I don't care if you got your doctorate at 20; Parvati got her's at 18."

Danny: "Who's she? Parvati?"

Justin: "Whiz kid from Mumbai. Wait until you meet her. You think *you're good…*" He grins at Danny, "You two have a lot in common. Ya ought to hit it off right away… if you make the team that is", he says with a wink.

During the Testing phase, there are several humorous scenes – especially when a candidate loses it during the Psych-Eval test. During the VR simulation, he gets rattled and begins yelling at other crew members to the point that he has to be calmed down, and they terminate the test for him.

Despite several minor issues, EPC schedules the lift-off 18 months after the RCSP – six months ahead of the originally planned schedule. The spaceship of the EPC, called the RSS-DT-1, will accommodate an 8-member crew.

After months of grueling tests, the ECP announced the crew for the RSS-DT-1 mission. Of course, controversy erupted over the US having two crew members, but considering the USA's overwhelming financial contribution to the project, opposition soon subsided.

The announced crew consists of:

Captain Justin Joiner (53) from the USA, chief pilot, cosmologist, and astrophysicist;

Andres Martin (39) from France, 2nd in command, pilot, technician, astrophysicist;

Daniel "Danny" Albright (21) from the USA, an astrophysicist and astrobiologist, discoverer;

Olivia Thomson (42) from England, IT wizard, programmer, communications, math tech;

Everett Becker (36) from Germany, chief engineer;

Yoshiro Sato (51) (♂) from Japan, a systems technician, solar sail designer, and engineer;

Parvati "Pari" Singe (24) (♀) from India, a biologist, biochemist, astrobiologist, programmer, and 3D animator;

Kwan Kim (46) (♀) from South Korea is a Chief Physician, virologist, chemist, and licensed psychiatrist.

Justin congratulates Danny on the appointment, "What did it for you was your doctoral dissertation. With your in-depth speculation of this possible extraterrestrial life, you may have nailed it before we even see the critters."

After several crew meetings, the team establishes a positive rapport with one another. The anticipation of an extraordinary adventure bonds them with much hope and enthusiasm. Danny and Pari hit it off immediately, having the same studies and both being early high achievers – he is smitten by her beauty and develops a secret crush on her. The team has a social gathering prior to launch day. Pari gets dolled up and looks stunning from her ordinary nerdy look with glasses and hair up. All the men can't help but admire.

The mission will include data and status updates to be sent to-and-from the RSS-DT-1 periodically along its 15-year journey to Alpha Centauri. With each transmission, a greater and greater gap will exist between send-and-receive times the further they go. Once they reach AC, it will take 4.3 years for transmissions to reach Earth.

There is intense interest and celebration for the Mission to Alpha Centauri. The nations of the EPC collectively rejoice in the lift-off. The event is a welcome distraction from the ongoing global ills tipping the world balance.

* * *

Fifteen Years Later

Fifteen years after lift-off, the DT-1 makes initial entry into Alpha Centauri's gravitational influence. The ship's proximity sensors initiate the computer to start activating the crew's return from cryo-sleep.

Captain Joiner is scheduled to revive from the cryo-sleep before the rest of the crew. After groggily stabilizing himself, his blurry eyes look about, and he is startled when he manages to detect a human figure in front of him. He can only barely voice, "Who… *who* is that?"

A male voice with an accent (sarcastically): "Hey Justin, you have looked better."

Justin can distinguish the accent, "Andres? Is that you? Thought *I* was due to be revived *hours* before everyone else."

Andres says, "I know (long sighs). Let us get you acclimated, and I'll tell you the whole story."

Later in the mess hall, the Frenchman explains that due to some malfunction in his cryo-hibernation system, the computer forced him to make an early out. He has now been out of hibernation for eight years. Justin is stunned. He continues, "We will have plenty of time for me to tell you my boring experience. But first, I must give you the sobering news." Andres briefs Justin as to the news from Earth and proceeds to show him several news feeds.

Justin somberly says to Andres, "Let me be the one to tell the crew about Earth."

Andres claps his hands and lightens the discussion by telling Justin, "Now for some good news, let me show you what we have come all this way to see," as he leads him to the main deck. Justin guzzles down the rest of his water and excitedly follows Andres.

Andres enters the main bridge where he has set up the large monitor with the focused, telescopic view of the shimmering sphere of swimming creatures. When Justin enters, he stops abruptly and just stares for a moment, while Andres just grins, enjoying the sight of the Captain's reaction. As Justin slowly steps toward the screen, he begins laughing. By the time his face is 12 inches from the screen, he is containing his sobbing with joy.

The visual is extraordinary in that millions upon millions of entities – living creatures - are now discernable. Individually, they look like large amoebas, clear bodies with several opaque objects within them – one large object as if a nucleus. Sparkles of prismatic light twinkle as the starlight is refracted through their ever-shifting, moving, undulating bodies. Justin is just in awe at the dazzling spectacle.

"Ya know, I could watch this for hours… make that days."

Andres: "I've been watching it for *years*. Just keeps getting better. And the closer we get, the more detail we will see. I will have to let you see my notes. About four months ago, I first started seeing the individual '*amoebas*,' he says with a grin.

Justin stays transfixed on the screen. "Yeah, *amoebas*. That's the best description yet. *Gargantuan* amoebas. And yes, I'd like to see your notes.

You figured out how big they are?" Andres: "Not yet. Perhaps when we get closer, I am sure."

Justin continues, "Just look at that. A creature that has somehow managed to adapt and live in space – free from planetary dependency. No home but space itself."

Andres: "I call it the Orbital Zone. Apparently, there exists a hospitable dimension capable of sustaining this life form. Thickness to be determined." He adds, "I think Danny nailed it with his dissertation. I'm sure he is right about them being photosynthetic creatures, also."

Justin: "Yes, they have to be. Unless there's something we haven't yet seen."

As he watches, there is an amassing of a large number of the creatures, causing a darkening spot on the overall sphere. Justin says, "There it is, just as we speculated. Now, to figure out *why* they do that." He ponders, "You realize if they did not do this amassing, with the darkening effect, we might not have ever detected them."

Andres points straight out of the front bridge window at the twinkling white dot ahead, seen with the naked eye. Andres grinning, "There it is, just ahead of us." Justin has to pull his focus away from the monitor to look.

Andres: "We will be right on top of it in three to four months." He turns back to the monitor, "Something else I want to show you." Andres zooms back the telescope so that the sphere is a 10-centimeter disc on the screen.

About 8" outside of the sphere, faintly can be seen an asteroid belt. Andres speculates, "Possibly, a planetary collision eons ago."

Justin simply says, "Fascinating."

Back in the cryo room, one by one, the remaining six DT-1 crewmembers make their awakenings. As each revives, they grab a water bottle placed by Justin and follow the sign directing them to *Go to the bridge*. As each crew member enters the bridge and sees the image of the creatures on the large screen, they become awestruck (except for Everett) – amusing Justin and Andres as they watch each react.

Justin excitedly asks Olivia, "Is Danny up yet?"

Without looking away from the screen, she says, "Yes, he just got out of his cryo-unit."

Justin races to the cryo-sleep room and waits for Danny to acclimate. Justin: "What's going on, buddy?"

As they enter the bridge, Justin has his hands over Danny's eyes until they are right in front of the big monitor. All the rest of the crew are there. "Here you go, buddy! Meet 'Danny's Things'! (laughs) There's your little 'bugs' you saw 27 years ago." The rest of the crew cheer.

Danny does a combination laugh-cry as he just takes in the spectacle. The other crew members voice congrats and pat Danny on his back.

Danny quips to the group, "And I'm gonna come up with a really good name. You know, one of the 28-letter scientific names."

Danny says, "Looks like they are in an Orbital Zone of Proxima C-Beta."

Justin and Andres look at each other and grin.

Danny, along with Olivia, Pari, Kwan, and Yoshiro, focus on the screen, pointing out the features and actions of the creatures.

Everett finds it all interesting but just doesn't have the enthusiasm of the scientists as he stands back to observe. Justin and Andres talk quietly between themselves near the entrance door.

Pari says, "This is a scientist's wildest dream! To study a creature totally different from anything we've known before." The others gazing at the monitor express their affirmations.

After giving the crewmembers plenty of time with their first look, Andres gives Justin a slow nod, and Justin says to the crew, "OK, we will have plenty of time to study our new alien friends. (he then changes to a somber tone) Right now, we're going to switch gears. I need you all to go to the mess hall. I have a very important announcement for all of you." As they exit the bridge, crewmembers give each other quizzical looks. Andres just looks downwards and avoids eye contact.

Once they are all gathered and settled around the mess table, Justin says, "First of all, the projected time was very accurate. It is now the year 2047, and it took 15 years to arrive. Andres has been awake from cryo-sleep for 8 years now." Several gasp as they look towards Andres. Justin continues, "Something to do with a malfunction of his cryo-unit. We can be thankful he is alive."

He glances at Everett and says, "Engineering, you've got your first assignment. (Looks at rest of group) You can get Andres' interesting story at another time… But now, I wish I had good news from Earth, but I do not. I have already seen the newsreels and know they have suffered another pandemic about 8 years ago – much worse than the Covid-19. Brace yourselves, 23.7 percent of Earth's population lost their lives, directly caused by this… (looks to Andres for confirmation), this CoVid-41." Andres nods.

Andres queues the news videos to play on the monitor in the room and says, "With an incubation period of 30-45 days, this made the pandemic of the early '20s look like a cakewalk."

After several newsreels, Justin says, "I have set up tablets at each of your sleeping quarters to check the latest confidential communique that would have been sent to each of you regarding family and loved ones. I know each of you will have your news to deal with, but I encourage all of you to talk about it. In fact, we should convene to have a group meeting to share our grieving and condolences. Some of you may want to grieve in private, which is understandable. But we all need to get over it in our own way and get back to the mission we are all on. Personally, I lost my ex-wife and one of my three adult children." After a long, silent pause, "You are dismissed. Oh, one last thing. Kwan is a licensed therapist in case you'd like to talk to someone."

Soon after all retreat to their separate quarters, sobbing and crying are heard from the hallway.

As would be expected, some lost an entire family, while others lost no one at all.

In the next couple hours, one by one, each crew member joins Justin and Andres sitting at the dinner table in the mess. After several express their grief and receive condolences from the others, the crew of 8 all join hands in solidarity and say a non-denominational prayer.

After several minutes of silence, Kwan breaks the ice and asks Andres with an upbeat tone, "So Andres, tell us, what was it like during the last 8 years?"

Andres lightens up and puts his hands together, "Well, the first couple of years were not too bad. I found plenty to occupy my mind with, reading, research, watching the video feeds sent from Earth." Looks at Danny, "I read your dissertation", while he nods. "This is going to be exciting. I even got into writing myself. (Pauses and sighs) But in the *next* two years, things started to get rough. The loneliness and depression started getting to me.

But then… No doubt, the highlight of my predicament was about four years ago when the RSS-DT-1 overtook the RCSP-1. That was some 1.2 light-years ago. I have been preparing for this moment for quite a while." He shows them a video he recorded when the two ships were nearly tandem with one another. "Wish I could have seen the look on their faces at EPC command center when they received this video." As the crew watches a sped-up version of the RCSP-1 being overtaken, they all let out a cheer as everyone is laughing and cheering.

Olivia takes a closer look and asks Andres, "Can we zoom in more?" Andres zooms in as much as possible, making the ship fill the screen. She says, "Odd that they don't have any lights blinking… in fact, I don't see any light indications at all. Have we received any status reports on the RCSP-1 up to this point?"

Andres: "No. The RCSP has remained secretive about its project. Ever since they separated from the ECP, they have been uncooperative and sharing nothing. Also, the ECP has sent no communiques regarding our mission to the RCSP."

Everett: "I bet they're hiding something. You know those damn commies."

There is silence as several of the crew glance at Everett and at one another.

Olivia: "Perhaps we should send them a transmission."

Justin: "Orders are to only communicate if they hail us first. When they start getting close, we'll need to revisit the protocol. The original projection was that they were going to arrive 2 years after us."

"If there are no other questions, I'd like to do a quick tour. I know you did one before we had lift-off, but it's been 15 years. You may have forgotten," he says tongue-in-cheek.

Justin takes the crew to the Research Control Room, equipped with 6 workstations, a master workstation with a large wall monitor, whiteboards, and a center conference table equipped with a high-resolution, 3D-holographic display.

Justin explains, "For the extent of the mission, we will all share this room to discuss what we know so far and share conjecture and speculation. Soon, we will set up monitoring 24/7 with rotational shifts to make sure we catch any possible unique behaviors of our new species."

One Month Later

In the Research room, Pari, Danny, Justin, Olivia, and Andres are each working on the computers. Although Andres is not a scientist per se, he was able to study enough during the last 8 years to qualify himself to 'talk the talk' and is now a valuable asset to the scientific research team. Each of the monitors has content showing graphics, charts, equations, etc. Whiteboards are covered with drawings, diagrams, bullet lists, and theories.

On the whiteboard, under the header NAMES, there is a list that the group has come up with potential names for the creatures. At the top of the list was Astrocytes, but it was struck out with the note 'used'. Seemed like the perfect name, but who knew it was the name of a type of nerve in the brain – well, Kwan knew from her neurological studies. Next was Xenomorph, but it too was struck out due to the use by a popular movie franchise that used the generic term for their specific creature. The group thought it was a very good descriptor but didn't want the association attributed to it. Next are Xenobios, Alphaxenos (or Alpha-X), Exo-Solar entities, Protist, and finally, what the group agreed on was Xenocytes, or X-cytes, for short. Homonym, "excites," which everybody seemed to like.

The next column on the whiteboard is ANATOMY, underneath the categories: Form, Size, Age, Origin, Composition, Sustenance, Propulsion, Life Cycle, Communication, Behavior, and Population.

- Resembles something between large amoebas and neuron cells with trans-morphic qualities;
- Size averages that of a large automobile;
- Larger 'boss' or leader X-cytes are rarely seen, twice as large as typical X-cytes;
- Origin possibly from a panspermia incident; asteroid(s) with spores in sustainable region;
- Sustenance comes from photosynthesis from the star – within the O-Zone (OZ);

- Bodies go dark when amassing – probably to absorb more light/heat/energy;
- Seemingly transfer electrostatic pulses from one another – communication?
- Tonality/density seems to heighten when they collectively amass, causing light occlusion;
- Can change opacity and become darker to absorb more solar for energy bursts;
- Propulsion - Electrostatic bursts act as booster jets;
- Individually/Colonization

On the large master workstation screen, it reads Optimal Zone – OZ, with some diagrams and graphs underneath the title. This is the topic the group is currently discussing at the center table.

The OZ - Optimal Zone.

- A hollow sphere with the OZ an outer layer, volume TBD (see Hollow sphere equations);
- Physical Boundary is hospitable and conducive to sustenance; TEMP: 0-100 Celsius;
- They discover that on rare occasions, one or several will swim beyond the zone and will freeze beyond the outer threshold, and fry beyond the inner threshold; (here is lively debate as to whether this is purely accidental or if intent is present)
- A slight orbital rotation axis due to the star;

Justin discusses the plans to launch a smaller, on-deck probe for closer examination of the X-cytes in a few weeks. Importantly, they seek to retrieve a biological sample.

They have established 24/7 monitoring by at least 2 crewmembers on rotational schedules so as not to miss any pertinent activity by the X-cytes. At this time, Yoshiro and Everett are currently assigned the watch. Everett often gets bored with the assignment and frequently excuses himself for breaks. Yoshiro has become somewhat of an apprentice to Everett, following him around and learning everything he can. Everett relishes the role and proves to be a good teacher.

Danny and Pari present to the other scientists their theory as to the origin of the species. "Most likely, our alien creatures are the result of a panspermia incident millions of years ago. Perhaps two asteroids, each containing the essential building blocks for life. Fungi, spores, plus the basic elements of carbon and water came together in this ideal area we are calling the Optimal Zone. Took millions of years, but with all those ingredients, right here in an ideal incubation zone, we've got life."

Several Days Later - The Incident

Pari and Everett are assigned the 24/7 monitoring of this particular shift tonight – called the "graveyard shift" because most are sleeping during this 6-hour segment.

Pari says, "Everett, I'm going to go grab a coffee from the mess. You want me to bring you back anything?"

At first, he says, "No thanks, I've got an energy drink already." But after some thinking, he gets up and follows her to the break room - he has been harboring a desire for her and figures he'll make his move.

In the break room, Pari exclaims, "What are you doing? You know that someone always needs to be in the control room."

Everett: "Oh, it'll be OK. Nothing ever seems to happen."

As Everett was hitting on Pari in the break room, a Proximity Alert began silently blinking on Everett's unattended monitor on the bridge.

Just then, both Justin and Danny arrive an hour early to relieve the two. They enter the control room and notice the alert. Justin yells, "What the hell's going on here?! Who's supposed to be in here?!"

Pari and Everett are both startled and race back to the control room. Justin grills Everett while Danny just gives her a look of disapproval.

Justin races over to the telescope controls to see if the approaching object is visible. Sure enough, there it is - a meteor is streaming towards the OZ.

Justin yells at Everett, "You're dismissed!" Justin gets on the PA system and says, "All scientific personnel report to the bridge ASAP… you are *not* gonna wanna miss this." Everett goes to the exit but can't leave out of curiosity about what is about to happen.

The four just stare with gaping mouths as the meteor pierces into and through the OZ, wiping out all X-cytes in its path. Hundreds, if not thousands, of X-cytes, are left in the wake of the passing meteor. Danny is up front, his face a meter from the main screen, as Pari comes over to join him and whispers, "Nothing happened. He just followed me to the mess hall and made advances towards me."

Danny whispers, "Don't worry about it; we'll talk later. Let's just watch this astonishing spectacle." He clasps her hand and gives a slight squeeze to assure her it's all good. Justin zooms in the camera into the impact site and examines the 'hole' left in the OZ.

The entire crew shows up, not just the scientists, as curiosity grips everyone. Danny and Pari step aside so everyone can see the image.

Andres looks at the screen and says, "What the hell just happened?"

Justin replays the recorded video of the moment of impact on an adjacent monitor so newcomers can witness the phenomenon.

Then, the most extraordinary thing happens…

The X-cytes closest to the impact site (that weren't destroyed) start transmitting communication signals to adjacent X-cytes until a network begins forming that starts taking shape and form. The alignment forms longitudinal lines that radiate from the initial impact site and begin stretching and extending across the circumference of the OZ. Nearly the entire population of creatures forms a "neural net" to communicate with the X-cytes on the opposite side of the OZ as if they are letting the other side of the OZ know the impending impact and exit location of the meteor. However, instead of clearing away, the X-cytes amass to an extraordinary degree.

Several witnessing the event murmur expletives and superlatives to express their astonishment, but most are quietly awe-struck by the massive scale of the phenomenon.

Danny suggests positioning the ship to better see the exit site of the meteor. In the meantime, the communication signal can be seen spreading to the opposite side of the OZ.

As more and more X-cytes amass at the other side of the OZ, Justin is confused, "What the hell are they doing?"

Kwan: "Won't thousands more get wiped out?"

Danny says, "I… I think they are going to trap… or *catch* the meteor. And something tells me they've done this before."

Pari: "I think you're right."

Yoshiro, already tapping away on a nearby computer, says, "Based on the trajectory and distance, I'd say we've got a couple of hours till exit impact – one hundred and twenty-eight minutes, to be exact. This will give us time to re-establish a new position of the RSS-DT-1 to better see it."

"Good time to go get your coffees and take your potty breaks. I'm sure you will not want to miss what happens. I will send the live feed to the Research room, and you can also pull up the recording of the impact moment for research analysis."

Justin and Andres stay on the bridge to re-position the DT-1 to a more optimal spot to see the exit location of the meteor while the other scientists go to the Research Lab.

Everett retreats to his quarters, still fuming from being reprimanded. He pulls out a flask concealed as a can of shaving cream and gets drunk.

It is T-minus-20 minutes till impact.

Danny, Pari, Kwan, and Olivia are in the Research room watching a 3D simulation of the impact, speculating as to what will happen when the meteor reaches the other side of the OZ. Several think it will blast through, while others believe the X-cytes will be able to contain the meteor.

Danny: "Keep in mind, we are about to witness for the first time something that this species has probably done many times before. They *know* what they're doing."

T-minus 1 minute

Everyone is at their stations except for Danny and Justin, who stand several feet from the large center screen. They have the DT-1 camera poised, focused, and zoomed in on the impact site.

Yoshiro, monitoring the calculations for impact, begins a countdown from 10. Just before he says 1, humongous electrical currents, like tremendous lightning bolts, surge from the epicenter outward along the longitudinal bands of the X-cytes.

The meteor is caught as if by a web or net. The netting bows as the meteor slows and comes to a halt. Thousands of X-cytes swarm the meteor. It looks like a slow-motion of thousands of ants devouring an apple but at a massive scale.

Justin attempts to zoom in but reaches the zoom-extent as they all watch a slightly blurry scene of the mass feeding frenzy.

Olivia, slowly shaking her head: "They're feeding on it. Can you imagine that? They must be breaking down the elements for consumption. And we thought the light was their only means of sustenance." She turns to Danny and jokes, "Bet you didn't see *that* coming." All he can say is "Fascinating."

Danny continued watching the impact area long after all the others had left the room.

He gets super sleepy and can barely keep his eyes open when he starts to see a specific X-cyte that keeps growing and growing. It gets to be 1000

% of its normal size and then begins flying toward the camera. When it hits the camera at great speed, Danny is jolted awake from his dream.

Just then, Pari enters the room and says, "Hey there, let's get you tucked into bed."

Danny: "Sounds great, Pari. Wait until you hear about this dream I had."

Pari: "Was *I* in it?"

"Well no… it about this X-cyte…"

She plays with him, "Oh, you and your X-cytes again. You know I'm getting jealous."

He looks up at her, and they both start grinning.

In the days following, Justin assigns Olivia to assemble a press-release video of the incident for transmission to Earth. While everyone is in the Lab, he instructs her, "Any of us here can assist you with materials. Let's make sure we include drawings and graphs to illuminate the world public."

While she is in the Research room editing the piece, Danny, Pari, and Kwan are reviewing the recordings and discussing the behaviors exhibited by the X-cytes during the meteor capture. They study how the X-cytes break down the meteor by concentrating electrical impulses down a single pseudopodium (leg) and pulverize the meteor - like an impulse jackhammer.

Just then, Olivia receives an alert regarding a communique from Earth. Upon reading the message, she gasps. The others look over and ask if everything is alright.

"It is a communique from Earth. Keep in mind this was sent 4.5 years ago. It appears the RCSP has finally opened up about an event that occurred with their ship. In 2037, when the RCSP realized the RSS-DT-1 was to overtake their ship, they attempted to send a programming modification to the ship's computer to divert energy to the auxiliary booster rockets to try to keep ahead of the ECP, with the hope of arriving before us."

At that moment, Justin pops into the Research room and pressingly asks Olivia, "Did you read… Oh, please continue" when he realizes she is speaking to the others.

She reads on, "In 2039, the RCSP Control received a message of a catastrophic system failure on the part of the computer. All communication ceased from that point on. They suspect the code had a flaw and put it in an infinite loop or cause the computer to lock up." She stops reading and looks at the others, "So the video Andres took of overtaking their ship was 2 years after they went silent."

Justin says, "Olivia, your suspicions were correct. (To the group) What that means is the RCSP-1 is a ghost ship, a derelict 100,000-ton object hurdling through space. We don't know if anyone is still alive on board if the life-support system failed or not. Calculation puts it at roughly 2 years until it arrives. The command has issued orders to try and make contact, if by any means possible, with the RCSP-1."

The Probe

The team begins planning the deployment of the probe, the Mini DT-1, for tomorrow. The intention is to garner some tissue samples from one of the frozen X-cytes. They determined that outside of the OZ where the meteor was captured – where many X-cytes were frozen – was a good place to find a specimen. Whether the X-cyte is dead or not is left to be determined. They also discuss the possible limitations of the 3-meter drill, and whether or not they will be able to reach the nucleus of the X-cyte they intend to sample.

Pari suggests that after the sample is taken, they use the probe to push a frozen X-cyte back into the OZ to see if it will 'recover' and come back to life. Justin agrees, but *after* they obtained the bio-sample.

That evening, Danny visits Pari at her quarters. He knocks softly on her door. She stops her zero-G Yoga session. She opens the door slightly. He whispers close to the opening, "It's our anniversary, Pari. It was 16 years ago today that we first met."

Pari giggled, "Silly, it has been only one year ago our time."

She lets him in. They get romantic. Things start getting hot and heavy.

He holds out the sanctioned ECP personal hygiene effects he brought with him. She laughingly does the same.

Danny jokes, "Let's use yours… I'm going to sell mine on eBay when I get back. Can you imagine what it'll be worth?"

Pari frowned, "Just for that remark, buster, we're using *yours!*"

They exchange lascivious stares while he slowly rips open his hygiene pack.

The day has come to deploy the small probe to try to get up close and obtain a tissue sampling from one of the X-Cytes, one of the key priorities of the mission. This is a big day for the team, and there is a full staff on hand, even Everett, to monitor the mechanical functions. Justin and Andres are on the bridge, while the rest of the crew are in the Research room.

The DT-1 is positioned in sight of one of the dozens of frozen X-cytes. They decided to focus on one of the smaller X-Cytes for their sampling.

Probe Deployment

All indications point to the proper functioning of the Mini-DT. The small bay door on the DT-1 opens, and the Mini is released. Andres puts his training to play. The controls allow him to maneuver to the selected X-cyte – one in which the nucleus appears close to the side – within reach of the 3-meter drill. Now, with the mini-DT camera in action, the team now has two screens with live video feeds.

The Bridge and the Research Lab are on an open mic to hear any comments from anyone. The Mini-DT slowly maneuvers toward a chosen X-cyte that is freely floating. The next 10 minutes are spent flying slowly around the X-cytes to examine its exquisite structure. Now seen in glorious detail, a very fine network mesh of 'nerves' extends to the outer surface membrane from the complex nucleus.

Andres first uses one of the extending claw arms to grab hold of the X-cyte. After several attempts, he gets a firm hold. With the second arm, he is able to get a good grip to begin the sampling process. He aligns the target nucleus in the drill sights. The telescopic, hollow tube saw begins drilling into the frozen X-cyte.

Everyone is riveted to the video feed from the probe.

Everett notices a red blinking alert on one of the screens. He nudges Yoshiro, who in turn taps on Olivia's shoulder. Olivia contacts the bridge about the abnormal amassing on the OZ – it is right underneath where the Mini-DT is getting the sample.

Justin tilts the DT-1 camera to better see. Sure enough, the X-cytes are amassing at the point closest to the probe.

Danny quips, "You think they're just curious?"

Kwan: "I hope you are right."

Justin: "I dunno, but let's try to expedite the process if possible. This amassing is making me nervous."

The drill is just about to penetrate the nucleus…

Then it happens…

There is a rushing and pushing from the outer X-cytes towards the middle of the crowd. This causes an outward bowing of the mass. It continues until there is an acute, parabolic extension outside the OZ in the direction of the probe. Despite the fact that leading X-cytes are frozen and killed off, underlying Xcytes continue the surge toward the probe. The extension extends far enough to reach the probe!

The probe is then engulfed by the protruding mass - And PULLED back into the OZ.

The entire crew is left stunned until someone says, "What the hell just happened?"

An exasperated Justin says, "We just lost our probe; that's what happened."

He puts his hand on his forehead and walks toward the bridge exit, "And there goes our sample."

In the Lab, Olivia: "Can you believe that just happened? What are these critters going show us next?" she says, perplexed. Pari, given any chance to rib Danny, looks at him and says, "I don't remember reading about *that* in your dissertation," with a grin.

He's too stunned to be amused. Eventually, he chuckles but then gets serious, "One of us will have to go out there to get the sample." She looks and frowns at him to suggest, 'Not you.'

Andres comments, "We lost the 3-meter... we will only be able to get a 30 to 40-centimeter sample with the handheld drill."

Danny: "We need to figure out how we can get a sample of the nucleus. A DNA discovery would be the ultimate."

Everett catches a distraught Justin before leaving the bridge and says hushed, "Captain, I may have a solution. There may be a complete second probe on the ship. I read the manual, and it said there is a storage bin containing every replaceable part. Maybe I can have something for you in, say, a week?"

Justin brightens up, "Please look into that. Let me know if you think we can have a second probe. Listen, there's no rush. Let's just make sure it works." Before leaving, he pats Everett's shoulder, "That would be great."

Back in the Lab, Kwan says, "Well, we have a new behavior to add to their repertoire. They can extend *beyond* the OZ involving group dynamics... even involving sacrificial teamwork. True altruism, in its most basic form."

Pari: "Certainly something to be admired."

Danny: "All the parts supplement the whole, which is the *organism* we call the OZ."

Except for Justin and Everett, everyone continues to watch as the colony attempts to break down the probe. Some of the X-cytes are 'electrocuted' when contacting the probe and are either stunned or killed. The probe gets passed deeper into the OZ until, eventually it is spit out on the inside threshold towards the sun. It slowly floats away.

Justin thinks alone in his cabin. Soon, he returns to the bridge and starts issuing commands, "Scientific team, start studying the video and add to our knowledge base of our friends. Oliva, please begin preparing an update report for Earth of the probe incident. Everett, Yoshiro, and Andres meet me on the bridge."

On the bridge, Justin and the three establish the next plan to retrieve a sample.

Everett reports he has discovered the storage bin with a complete backup of the probe. He assures Justin that he is confident he can assemble a second probe with the help of Yoshiro.

This becomes Plan A. Plan B is to have someone go out to retrieve the sampling.

Way off in the asteroid belt, there is a collision of two boulder-sized entities sending shards in all directions, including towards the Oz.

While Oliva is in the Lab typing away at her incident report to send to Earth, Danny, Pari, and Kwan are examining the video of when the probe is pulled back into the OZ. Andres is also in attendance out of curiosity.

Questions on the whiteboard:

- How far beyond the OZ can they extend?
- What do they do with their frozen compatriots once pulled back?
- Via what sensory method were they able to "see" the probe?
- Are they hypersensitive to non-native entities within proximity?
- How were they able to calculate the exact distance for extension to capture the probe?

From the video, Danny points out that the X-cytes attempt to revive a frozen fellow by "zapping" it with energy jolts. Sometimes, it works, but most of the time, it does not. When unsuccessful, they push the dead one towards the inner boundary of the OZ, towards their sun. They find it comforting that the X-cytes do not resort to cannibalism.

While looking at the control menu, Andres then discovers a secondary probe camera that wasn't patched into a monitor earlier. It shows the extraordinary POV video during the capture and subsequent breakdown attempts by the X-cytes in the OZ – from the perspective of the probe. The scientists are enthralled by the spectacle of seeing X-cytes generate electrical bursts that are directed at the probe. After 6 shots, the camera signal begins to deteriorate - by a dozen zaps, it is completely disabled.

Justin enters the room and initially shows interest in the discussion. However, when given the opportunity, he changed the subject to discuss the plans. He lays out Plans A and B to the crew.

Several immediately volunteer to do the sampling in the event of Plan B, including Danny, Andres, and even Pari – when she sees Danny volunteer. They both give disapproving looks to each other.

Justin: "Duly noted. But before jumping ahead to Plan B, let's invest more faith in Plan A with the Probe-2."

Near the end of the meeting, Olivia announces a communique has been received from Earth. "Hey gang, get a load of this. The RCSP council is granting *permission* to attempt any COMM-link with their ship's computer. There will be a subsequent message to supply the details for System-Link protocol."

Justin was surprised, "Wow, I didn't see that coming. What do we have, 18 months till they arrive?"

Andres: "Yes, according to the last projections when they lifted off."

Olivia continues, "Well, listen to *this*, the RCSP believes that some of the booster ignition commands may have *partially* executed before the system failure. In other words, it may get here *before* 18 months from now."

Yoshiro adds, "We will need to set up a proximity detection radar in the direction of the RCSP-1 to get the earliest detection."

Andres: "Good idea. We will need to know as soon as possible what our timeframe for the RCSP-1 arrival will be."

Everett and Yoshiro soon rig a dedicated radar dish on the outer hull, pointed back towards Earth to pick up the incoming RCSP ship.

After a week, Everett successfully builds the second probe with assistance from Yoshiro. The two test it as thoroughly as possible. They are ready to deploy. Everett relishes the notion that he has come through 'to save the day.'

Probe II Deployment

Andres is controlling the probe toward the X-cyte, everything seems to be going fine. Then, a malfunction occurs – it is unable to stop. He keeps pulling back on the control stick, but the probe continues its forward motion.

Everett demands, "Pull back!"

The Probe crashes into the X-cyte, crushing the control arms of the probe used to stabilize for drilling. The probe bounces back as the large X-cyte barely moves.

Everett blows up and blames Andres, calling him "dummkopf," and storms off the bridge.

The crewmembers are all numb, having just witnessed another setback in their attempts to obtain a sample.

Andres looks at Justin and just holds up his hands, shakes his head, and says, "The probe just lost communication. What could I do?" Justin: "Don't worry, it's not your fault."

Before leaving the bridge to follow Everett, Justin instructs Andres and Yoshiro to retrieve the damaged probe. "We need to get that 3-meter drill from the unit."

Justin meets with Everett in his quarters, calms him down, and gets him rational. Everett apologizes and admits he has screwed up several times but now wants to redeem himself with the rest of the crew. He pleads to be the "sampler" for Plan B.

Justin: "I dunno… You are too valuable here. I can't go with that plan."

Everett: "I have been training Yoshiro; he knows just about everything he needs to know about the ship."

Justin: "Let me give this some thought."

Everett pleads, "Please, Captain. I *need* this."

Justin, after some thought: "OK, I see how important this is for you, and you certainly have the determination. We will go forward with you for Plan B."

Andres and Yoshiro successfully retrieve the probe-2 using the tethered line and place it in the airlock; they keep it quarantined for 24 hours – dousing it with ultraviolet light.

The Scientific Team is excited they are able to at least get tiny ice fragments from the probe to analyze.

Everett and Yoshiro proceeded to extract the extension drill and build a hand-held mechanism.

Three Days Later

Justin, Andres, and Yoshiro help get Everett prepared for his mission. The brief and re-brief him on protocols taught during the pre-flight training for spacewalks. First and last rule: DO NOT PANIC.

They pick a frozen X-cyte well beyond the OZ freezing threshold - twice the distance from the OZ than the probe that was snatched.

Everett maneuvers his way to the lone frozen X-cyte using the tether cable. He fastens himself to it and begins the drilling.

A large 'leader' X-cyte begins communicating with the general population in the OZ closest to where Everett is working. A crowd slowly begins amassing. Everett can hear over the intercom someone say something that looks concerning. Everett: "What is going on?"

Everett looks towards the OZ and gets nervous as the amassing grows threatening.

Justin reassures Everett he is far enough away to avoid a snatch attempt.

Unexpectedly, some space debris from the asteroid belt knocks into the X-cyte while Everett is still drilling, pushing both Everett and the X-cyte toward the OZ. Everett continues the drilling, but the mission now becomes perilous as they slowly float closer to the OZ. The amassing starts getting dark and ominous. The drill saw is near to the nucleus. He is determined to get it despite Justin ordering him to extract and return to the mothership immediately.

He reaches the nucleus with the drill. The X-cytes are appearing to attempt another snatch; he must be nearing their range of extension. Everett has trouble extracting the drill. He pulls and pulls; finally, he puts both feet on the X-cyte to try and yank the drill from the creature. Everyone aboard the ship is riveted to the monitors, most urging him on, others saying prayers.

Everett can't help himself; he looks down at the OZ and sees the rushing of X-cytes towards the center of the mass.

Just then, the drill comes loose from the X-cyte and Everett thrusts away with the drill in hand. The crew all gasped.

The rushing, protruding mass envelops the area he occupied just seconds ago – and merely meters away.

Everett yelps; he is in shock but soon orients himself to return to the ship. The relief he feels is ineffable. He alternates between laughing and crying, depending on whatever thought is in his head. He can hear the entire crew applaud him. He jokes, "As they say, it looks like the *third time is the charm*."

Everett enters the decompression airlock. He places the sample in the 3-meter-long quarantine tube, which has basic compositional analysis tools built into its shell casing.

When Everett exits the airlock, it seems the crew is more concerned for the sample than for Everett's wellbeing. He sarcastically "You are welcome… And I am OK, thank you… thank you!"

The group acknowledges their lack of concern and thanks Everett on his perilous yet successful mission.

The Sample Study

Danny and Pari analyzed the sample using the built-in tools of the quarantine tube. The drill sample was able to traverse a multitude of various tissues of the X-cyte, although 90% of the sample is endoplasm.

Overall, the chemical composition closely resembles that of the simple amoeba – even down to its DNA.

However, they discovered a small, bulbous tissue appending to the outside of the nucleus, which, upon chemical analysis, confirmed by Kwan, to resemble brain-like matter. This opens up many speculations as to how this may affect their behavior, with possible decision-making capabilities.

For the X-cytes, the nucleus acts as an energy storage vessel that fans outward to the outer ectoplasmic membrane, not unlike a central nervous system.

Later that night, Danny wakes up from a nightmare where their sample comes to life, breaks out, and starts terrorizing the crew. He tells Pari, "I watched too many alien sci-fi movies growing up." Pari adds, "Yes, you notice nearly all of them end up tragic and horrific? Makes people fearful of the unknown." Danny: "Well, that's entertainment for you."

Justin and Olivia receive a significant message from Earth: the RCSP sends the initiating link code, protocol instructions, and passwords. They are also given the full mainframe source code along with the initial command code that brought on the system failure. In addition, all of the RCSP-1 schematics are delivered to assist in boarding and any possible maintenance.

The research room is filled with the entire crew, and they peruse the documents.

Yoshiro comments, "You know this was very difficult for the Russians and Chinese to release this to us. Their desperation must be epic to ask for our assistance in this way."

Justin: "It's understandable when we're talking about a possible three trillion dollar salvage mission."

Olivia and Pari begin examining the code, which is a mixture of C, C++, Assembly, Java, and Python. They both begin referencing manuals as refreshers to decipher the code.

Andres joins in the coding party. He jokes with the other two, "I got two degrees in computer programming in the eight years I was waiting for you guys to wake up," he says with a grin.

After days of tedious scouring of the code by the three, Andres is the one who makes the discovery. He finds that the command code sent to attempt the booster-ignition re-rout had a deep subroutine that stepped on an obscure database variable that was used in the primary master program. That one little mistake caused the system failure, leading to a very expensive project gone awry.

The three feverously work the code to reinitialize and correct the variable and obtain an open-link communication to the RCSP-1 computer. Countless attempts are made, and once it seems futile, a link is established with code made by Olivia. She yells, "I have comm-link!" Both Pari and Andres simultaneously kiss her cheeks. The three just stare glowingly at the prompt, waiting for a command.

They report to Justin and the rest of the crew of the great news. A collective cheer is shared by the ECP crew. It is a great bonding moment.

Proximity detection puts the RCSP as just entering the furthest gravitational reaches of the red dwarf.

Within several days, they are able to issue commands to the RCSP-1 computer, directing it to initiate reverse boosters and decelerate the ship.

The RCSP comes to a stop approximately 200,000 KM away from the RSS-DT-1.

Boarding the RCSP

Plans are made to assemble a rescue/salvage team to rendezvous with the derelict ship and board it.

The full crew has a meeting in the mess to plan the mission. The team of Justin, Kwan, Everett, and Andres plan to board the ghost ship.

The rest of the crew will monitor the team from the Lab. Yoshiro studies the RCSP-1 schematics to navigate the team to the bridge, while Olivia prepares the computer instructions once the bridge computer is accessed by the team.

Days later, they get close enough to establish a 90-meter tether line to the RCSP.

It is a very apprehensive scene when they board the RCSP-1. The interior is iced over, as the environmental system ceased along with the gravity-stabilization system. As they float through several rooms in the hull, there is a very fine mist in the air that causes their flashlights to cast visible beams across the room. Justin uses the expandable screen film on his forearm to access the ship's map. They make their way to the bridge to access the command computer terminal.

As Andres positions himself in front of a ready computer screen, Olivia reads the commands for Andres to type into the computer in Russian: "Restore ENV Suitability Conditions."

Back at the RCSP ship, intense apprehension is felt during their venture to the cryostasis room. What to expect? Is the crew still alive, or has this been a floating tomb for the last 3 years?

Kwan kneels and wipes the frost from the dim vitals indicator on one of the units.

She sighs deeply, "This one is still alive."

The others quickly do the same to the remaining units. One by one, "Alive!" is heard.

There is intense relief when the cryostasis units are found to be working - and all are still alive.

Andres uses the RCSP instructions to initiate the cryostasis release of the ship's crew.

Andres says, "It will take an hour or two until they start reviving. Let us find their mess hall. I want to see if they have some French roast coffee," he quips. The others just grin and follow him.

After about 30 minutes, the ship's EV System has achieved stable and comfortable conditions of temperature and oxygen levels. Oh, and Andres found the coffee he was looking for.

The ECP crew welcomes the RCSP crew as each awakens from cryostasis with a robe and hot coffee or water. Of course, each has a surprised and confused look as they see the ECP crew. Kwan uses the hand-held translator to assure them everything is all right, and when everyone is revived, there is a long story to be told.

Later, the full RCSP crew are sitting in the mess listening to Justin and Andres describe the events leading up to today – including the ordeal of the RCSP-1 and the pandemic back on Earth.

* * *

Eventually, both missions are fused into one, as complete disclosure leads to full-on collaboration and trust of all nationalities. The ECP scientists show their RCSP counterparts the discoveries to date while the engineers share systems information. (Great montage of sharing scenes between the mingling teams.)

Narrator, with God-like voice:

"And so, the scientific teams of the opposing missions work together in cooperation, trust, and earnestness to develop the most thorough analysis of the first known extraterrestrial entities, known as Xenocytes.

(Pause) Well, I know what you're thinking, that I was going to say that deceit and mistrust crept in and made a calamity of the mission. But no - That didn't happen. This one ended well.

The combined research and collaboration ushered in a new age of biological and astrological understanding that opened the door to the possibilities of extraordinary species only defined by our imaginations and dreams.

Just before the ECP crew settles into cryo-sleep, Danny and Pari tie the knot, with Justin presiding in a delightful ceremony.

Now, both the RCSP and the RSS-DT-1 are on their long journeys home. All crews are in restful cryo-sleep with hopes that the nations of Earth are at peace with one another when they return."

THE END

Lucy & Henry

Bruce Clark Bennett ©2021

It is morning, and Lucy is tight on time, getting ready to leave. She rushes around the upscale apartment, collecting her books and classwork, preparing to go to graduate school class for Abnormal Psychology. She shares the apartment in the metropolitan city with Jack, her fiancé, who is an intern doctor at a suburban hospital. The good-looking couple met in pre-med and plan to marry once he establishes residency at the hospital. She has a waitress job at a fine restaurant a few nights a week for some extra cash. He is under a lot of pressure during the internship and has been demanding of Lucy and, at times, exhibits demeaning and derogatory language towards her. She has learned to compartmentalize and rationalize the subtle verbal abuse due to the pressures of his internship.

Lucy's class assigns onsite fieldwork at participating local mental sanitariums to interview schizophrenic patients - this semester's focus. Due to funding, this is the first time in eight years this has been included in the university's curriculum. For the next four weeks, she will be scheduled to do interviews on Tuesdays, Wednesdays, and Thursdays at 11 a.m. at a suburban facility named Pleasant Valley Care (PVC). Weekly reports are expected for both the professor and the chief psychologist at the facility.

Week 1

On Monday, Lucy is to meet for orientation with the PVC chief staff psychologist, Dr. Bertrand Brown, to receive her case files. Needless to say, these are cases from Dr. Brown's 'dead folder', meaning he has virtually given up on getting through to these patients for some reason or another. Her intro discussion is not without flirtatious innuendo from Brown. Being an attractive young woman, she is wise to this type of suggestive talk and is able to thwart Dr Brown's subtle advances and keep the conversation focused in a polite way. As he tosses the first file in front of Lucy, he gives a brief synopsis of the case:

"Christina. Asian female, 42, a catatonic schizophrenic who has completely withdrawn from reality. Attempts have been futile in getting her to communicate on even the most basic level. Immature Psychosexual development and raped by an uncle at the aged 16. In her mid-20s, she tried to initiate a date with a male friend but was spurned and mocked by him. This drove her into a deep depression and social withdrawal that developed into her current condition." Changes his tone, "Good luck trying to get through to her – it's like talking to a vegetable."

He tosses the next folder, "D'shawn. Black male, 29, a paranoid schizophrenic who is prone to either externalize or internalize violent behavior. In his teens, he got a bullet to the head in a gang-related firefight and lost 20 percent of his brain tissue in the surgery. That started the dynamic bipolar behavior that developed into his current condition. There is a list of trigger words that you will want to *avoid* while talking with him. I assure you, there will be an orderly present for ALL these sessions, not just with D'shawn. Frankly, sometimes you don't know what to expect from these people."

"And for the third case we have…" Brown picks up two folders off the desk and juggles between them and says, "Eeny, meeny, miny, moe," then holds one up. She hides her contempt that he would treat the choice so frivolously. "Looks like we have..." Looks at the file tab, "Henry… Caucasian male, 26, multiple personality - your classic Dissociative Identity Disorder. D-I-D. You *do* know about those, right?" he says in a condescending tone. She just looks up from reading and nods. She then asks a follow-up question that proves she knows quite well. He fumbles for an answer.

Dr. Brown continues, "Henry had an extreme, traumatic experience at age 11. Home invasion by escaped cons. Tortured and killed his parents and sister in front of him… they tortured Henry for hours until police did a welfare check on the family by request from a neighbor. Was catatonic for several years and then started exhibiting multiple personalities in his early teens. He was pigeonholed in some sanitarium for nine years before he landed here. (He changes tone) He's all over the place. I lost count of the different personalities after 30. Although, at one time, he claimed he could control which personality would be prominent, but I know he's just *conning* me."

A puzzled Lucy, "What do you mean 'conning you'?"

Brown, matter-of-factly, "He can control his personalities no more than I can control the weather. He's pretty smart. He had a calculated IQ of 124 at age 11 before the trauma. So he is very clever. If he thinks he can get out of here by saying that, he's got another thing coming. Not on my watch, anyway." She just looks up at him stoically but thinks to herself, he's got a lot of contempt for this Henry.

They wrap up the meeting. As she is collecting the folders to take with her, he can't help but slip in one last suggestive innuendo. She just ignores it and says, "See you tomorrow at eleven, Dr. Brown."

That night, after dinner with Jack, she reads, in-depth, the files of her three patients. He is watching a sports game on TV, just chilling and decompressing from the day. They haven't talked much lately.

The following day, Lucy is shown to a small meeting room that has one window and two doors opposite each other. She is to begin her first interview with Christina, who is already seated at the table. Despite Lucy's best efforts, they get nowhere. She tries in vain to get Christina to make eye contact but to no avail. She begins reading Christina's file in detail to find any triggers that might help get through to her. The one-hour session seems an eternity.

The next day, Lucy interviews D'Shawn. For the first 20 minutes or so, she seems to make good rapport, but then, she unknowingly uses a *new* 'trigger phrase' that enrages D'Shawn. He leaps across the table and tries to strangle Lucy. The first orderly manages to separate the two, but it takes several orderlies to restrain D'Shawn and get him under control. They quickly shuffle him back to his room and lock him up while a nurse is attending to Lucy, still on the floor, gasping for breath and rubbing her neck. Despite saying she is okay, they roll the ambulance for her.

Lawyers representing the University contacted Lucy that evening. They ask her if she wants to press charges, but she declines.

Thursday, Lucy had a discussion with Dr. Brown before entering the interview with Henry. She is wearing a medical neck collar due to yesterday's incident. Brown assures her that D'Shawn is off the table and she will not have to face him again. He and the facility are worried Lucy will bring a lawsuit against Pleasant Valley Care.

Lucy enters the interview room, where Henry is seated at a blank table. She sets up at the table with a notepad and pen. She smiles an unnatural smile forced by the brace and begins, "Hello. Sorry to keep you waiting. Who do I have the pleasure of speaking with at this time?"

Henry looks at watch, "Oh, you got Henry now. It's 11:12."

Lucy: "What do you mean?"

"Between 11 and 12:30, I'm Henry."

"So. At 12:30, you become someone else. And you know who it's going to be?"

Henry, matter-of-factly, "Sure. It'll be Sonya."

She does a slow nod and says, "And how long have you been becoming Sonya, at precisely 12:30 daily?"

Henry looked up, pondering, "About four weeks now. That's when I started my new story."

Lucy: "Your *story*… so you are a writer?"

"Yeah, I got the bug to write about five years ago." Henry looks at Lucy's neck, "So what's with the neck brace?"

"Oh, well, I met D'Shawn yesterday."

"Ahhh… Yeah. A couple of years ago, I just asked him something about his mom and he went ballistic on me. Put me in the medical ward for three days. I stay clear of him, as do most everyone else."

"Yes, good idea. I don't blame you. I've heard through the grapevine that they are going to send him to a more secure facility. Henry, back to your claim, you say you can control which alternative personality is prevalent at the time?"

"The *Alters*, as I call them. Well, to some degree. Up until 5, 6, or 7 p.m., I can control the Alters. But later in the evening, I don't know who has manifested. By the time I sleep, I have no idea who I am." He pauses and puts thought into his next statement, then says confidently, "I can't remember the Alters that I don't control."

"How many characters are in your latest book?"

"Six for now. But I plan on adding at least two more."

Lucy, incredulously, "So you are controlling six alternative personalities at this time?"

"Yup."

"Can you tell me all their names? …and what they are like?"

"Well, as I mentioned, there is Sonya. Then Bobby, Ralph, Caitlyn, Shirley, and Demitri.

After a lengthy pause, "So, tell me about Sonya."

"She is a fun-loving teenager who likes the typical things a teenager likes, particularly anime." He goes on to describe Sonya's appearance, lifestyle, and place in the story he is writing.

After pausing and looking at her notes, she looks up at Henry and says, "Why didn't you ever tell Dr. Brown about this?

"Well… I *did* some time ago. But he just dismissed it – said I was just making that up to get out of here. Talk about a 'Catch-22', eh?" he says with a wink. "Anyways, I just don't particularly like the guy. At times, while talking to me, I see he's paying more attention to his hot sports car parked outside the window. Or I catch him ogling the nurses walking to their cars. He doesn't pay attention. He just wants to pigeonhole me in a textbook schizophrenic category and move on. He calls me a D-I-D."

"But you could get out here if you show them you can control your Alters."

"Where would I go? What would I do? I like it here. It's predictable; people are friendly with me, and everything is provided for me. All I have to do is B.S. to Dr. B," he says, grinning.

After a long pause, a very puzzled Lucy asks, "B.S.? What do you mean by *B.S.*?"

"Yeah… I'll just make up an Alter when he talks to me. It's kinda funny when I think about it." Henry looks away and grins but then gets serious and, with wide eyes, looks at Lucy, "But don't tell him! I'm sure he'd get really pissed off if he knew. Anyways, he hardly ever talks to me anymore, maybe once every other month or so."

"When you BS with him, do you pick an Alter from your story to fake with Dr. B?"

"No, usually I make up some weird character," he chuckles. "I just love to see him get that look on his face when he is totally confused." Henry mimics the frowning, confused look while Lucy tries to hold back a laugh.

He goes on to explain that when he was at a previous sanitarium, orderlies would set him down in front of the TV to occupy himself. Show after show, hour after hour – all day long.

"I would mimic the characters. At the top of the hour, a different show, different characters. I would become those characters. The clock would become my trigger. Though I would always get grounded with Henry at 11 a.m."

"Eleven AM, hmm? And why was that?"

"…'cuz that's when lunch was served!" he says with a grin. They both share a chuckle. "Several years ago, I got the impetus to write my own stories. I stopped watching TV and just started writing. Because my brain was already wired for it, I would go to a different personality at a specific time. All of whom were in the story I was writing at the time."

"How many stories have you written?"

"Oh, about a couple dozen. The early ones were rather short stories. But they've become longer as time goes on."

Lucy coaxed, "May I read one of your stories?"

Henry quickly looks at her but then cowers, "Oh, I don't… I don't think so. I don't think you'd like my stories."

Lucy frowns, "Why do you think I wouldn't like them, Henry?"

He looks away, "Aww, I'm just an amateur. You would think them so naïve… or worse, boring."

Very reassuring, "How about I be the judge of that." She leans to get his eye contact, "So, next time, you bring one of your recent stories and let me read a little bit." She motions a small amount with her fingers. "Just a little bit." He makes eye contact and shyly laughs with a grin.

Henry nodded, "Yeah, OK, I just might do that." He looks away and then shyly looks at her, "I like you. I wish you were my shrink rather than Doctor B over there." He points at Dr. Brown in the parking lot, showing off his new exotic sports car to a new nurse on staff. Henry looks at his watch, "Well, time flies; it's noon. I need to write a bit before Sonya takes over. Looks like we'll pick up with this next week."

Lucy glances at her watch with surprise, "Well, It was a pleasure meeting you today, Henry. I look forward to our next meeting… and reading one of your stories next week", she says with a smile.

Henry enthusiastically said, "Yeah, me too." He nods and waves with an innocent grin.

Back home that evening, Lucy can't stop thinking about her conversation with Henry as she is doing her daily routine of making dinner for Jack and herself. They don't talk much lately. He prefers to decompress by binge-watching TV while she is busy with schoolwork.

That night, Lucy and Jack are having sex, doggy-style, when she looks to the side of the mirror and can see he is on his phone during the act. She pulls away and turns to catch him red-handed with a phone. "What the *fuck*?!"

Jack sheepishly, "I was checking to see if the hospital paged me or not. Sorry, baby." She knows by now when he is not telling the truth. They have a bad argument and he sleeps on the couch that night. Before sleeping though, he gets back on his phone to do some texting.

On Friday morning, Dr. Brown calls Lucy to find out if she wants to choose a different case in place of D'Shawn and suggests the fourth file. Brown is on his best behavior, as he wants to please Lucy and dissuade her from any lawsuit. Lucy convinces him that rather than see a new patient; she would prefer to do two sessions a week with Henry. He agrees, so long as the school class instructor is cool with it.

After the call, Brown mutters to himself, "Well, looks like that little pissant has got *her* fooled."

Later that day, Brown meets with Henry to discuss meeting with Lucy twice a week. At first, Henry is disappointed that he will lose the time Wednesday that he would normally spend writing, but as he thinks of his enjoyable talk with Lucy, he changes his mind and expresses interest in doing so.

On the weekends, Lucy does full 8-hour shifts at the Primrose restaurant and sometimes does overtime when called for. The tips are great at this high-priced French eatery. One of her waitress-coworkers - a good friend and classmate - works at a strip club across town and tries to convince Lucy she could make a lot more money doing the same, with her good looks and all. But she steers clear of having that potential skeleton in her closet. Besides, Jack wouldn't approve, and her parents would be appalled if they found out.

Week 2

Monday, during class reviews, Lucy convinces the teacher in private to let her have two sessions a week with Henry. The teacher is skeptical that a DID would be able to control personalities but agrees to let her double her sessions with Henry. She sees Lucy's passion and enthusiasm with the patient Henry. Besides, she is interested in seeing how this will progress.

Lucy, quite aware she has the upper hand with Dr. Brown and the PVC, negotiates with the facility that she could get Henry to open up more if she interviews him in his room – of course, with Henry's approval.

Dr. Brown pops in on Henry and asks him if it is alright for Lucy to meet him in his room. Henry turns and says, "Sure" - this coming from whichever alter is currently manifest in Henry at 3:20 pm. Dr. Brown sends Lucy an email granting permission to meet with Henry in his room, that is, with an orderly just outside the door. He already has a desk in his room for the two to sit at for their session.

Tuesday

Lucy's neck is feeling better, and goes without the brace now. She brings with her some basic psychological association images to try to get through to Christina. Lucy has some slight progress with her as she manages to get her to glance, even for a moment, at any of the illustrations. A dozen out of a couple hundred is progress. Lucy later examines the pictures that Christina responded to, looking for correlations.

Wednesday

When Lucy arrives at PVC, she is escorted to Henry's room. When they get to the door, the orderly verbally reviews the protocol memo. Lucy listens but is more interested in peering into the window to get a read on his domicile, which is very sparse and simple. He has several bookshelves lined with a variety of books, a single twin bed, a dresser, and a table and chair.

Henry greets her with a goofy but sincere smile. An extra chair is brought in for Lucy by the orderly and placed next to the table.

Henry is noticeably anxious, so Lucy makes sure Henry is comfortable with her being in his space. He has never had a female other than the staff in his room. Lucy talks to Henry in a very comforting and reassuring tone to get him to acclimate to the situation.

After about 15 minutes, he begins to feel more at ease to open up and share. She brings up the plan they discussed last week to let her read his story. After another 10 minutes of coaxing, Lucy finally gets Henry to agree to let her read from one of his composition books. He goes over to his dresser, looks into the second drawer, and cautiously pulls out a composition book from underneath some clothing. He cautiously brings the comp book over to the desk and slowly slides it towards her. She senses his trepidation and mollifies the situation by assuring him with encouraging talk.

He watches her intently while she begins reading. After a few minutes, he grabs a nearby composition book and begins writing. She soon catches on that it is a pulp-fiction romance. Periodically, he cautiously glances up at Lucy to see her reaction. He grins slightly when he sees her eyes light up while reading. She stops several times to laugh and looks at Henry. Inside, he is thrilled to see someone react to his stories – something he has never had the pleasure of experiencing before, for she is the first person to read his stories.

Later, she hears her timer beep as they reach the end of the hour session, and she is only a quarterway through his story.

"Henry, I am very impressed! Your depth of insight and empathy for each of the characters is fascinating." She flips through the remainder of the book. "May I take it home with me to finish? I can have it back to you tomorrow," she says in a coaxing voice.

Startled, Henry exclaims, "OH… No, no, I can't let them out of my room."

She thinks for a moment. "Henry, how about I leave you something that is very valuable to me so you can be assured I will return it? It would be tomorrow."

He ponders the offer, "I dunno… Hmm. What did you have in mind?"

She looks in her purse at first, then glances at her engagement ring. At first, she is tentative but then slips it off. "Henry, how about this?"

After gasping, Henry says, "Are you sure?"

"Yes, but don't lose it," she says with a grin.

"Yeah, I know just where to put it." He gently takes the ring and puts it in the second dresser drawer under several shirts.

He feels insecure watching her put his comp-book in her case. She says, "I'll have it back to you tomorrow", with a reassuring smile. He is easily calmed and amenable by her good-natured smile.

As she is packing up her notes, Henry asks "Who else are you seeing here at Pleasant Valley?"

"I'm also seeing Christina."

"Oh yeah… she's a catatonic, isn't she?"

"That's right, she is. I'm having trouble getting through to her. She just sits and stares off into the distance. I have tried a lot of things to break through, but nothing has worked. "

He ponders for a moment, "You might want to try *anime*. One time in the community room, I noticed her looking up at the TV when a Japanese cartoon was on. It's the only time I ever saw her focus on anything."

"Huh. Thanks. I just might try that in my next meeting with her."

They bid one another fond farewell – even though they are seeing each other the next day.

At home, Lucy reads Henry's story and is astounded at the quality of his writing. She is forced to look up several words because of his adept vocabulary.

At 7:30 pm over at Pleasant Valley, Henry is Dexter - an impetuous late teen. He is in the middle of a chess game in the rec room with another resident named Burly-Hurley. With a mouth full of soda, Dexter blurts out a laugh at Hurley's new move and drenches his shirt. While Hurley is laughing back at Dexter for his gaffe, Dexter gets up, points at the board game, and says, "Don't move a single piece!" And then races to his room. At the dresser, he quickly yanks a shirt from the second drawer. Unknowingly, Lucy's ring springs out of the drawer and takes a queer bounce into the underside ledge of the bed frame, hidden from view. He slams the drawer quickly and changes his shirt on the way out of the room. The oblivious Dexter, with a new dry shirt, returns to the rec room and inspects the board before sitting back down. He claps once, then wringing his hands, he looks at Hurley and says, "OK, big man, where'd we leave off?"

Back at Lucy's, she is reading the last chapter of Henry's story in bed. Jack decides to have sex, but she says she's not in the mood. They haven't had sex since she caught him with the phone the last time.

It is around midnight when she finishes. She shakes her head and clicks her tongue in astonishment at how good his story is. While Jack is snoring away, Lucy gets up from bed and goes to the office. On the desktop computer, she begins researching the publishing process and possible publishers.

Thursday

The following day, when Lucy returns with his book, she finds him busy at the desk, feverously writing in a composition book. He surprises her by requesting several minutes to finish writing his thoughts. As she stands quietly, she is annoyed at first but quickly realizes *let him write – he has a gift*.

She lauds him about the story and characters. He humbly receives the kudos. After discussing characters and plot for a while, she slides the comp book towards him and looks up at him. He doesn't catch on immediately that it is his turn to retrieve her collateral. He says, "Oh yeah!" He is smitten with her, and at times, she catches him with a meandering mind. He dons that smile, then grins and gets up to walk to the dresser.

He goes to get the ring, but he can't find it and begins to panic. Lucy remains stoic but feels her blood pressure starting to rise while she watches

Henry nearly get hysterical. He flings all the shirts and underwear from the drawer onto the floor. He pulled out all his comp books and leafed through them for the ring. After the second drawer is emptied, he checks the other three drawers. She tries to console him from panicking.

He slinks down in a fetal position and sobs. Then he starts hitting his head with his hands. She tries to calm him to avoid a psychotic break, while in the back of her head, she is wondering about the consequences of losing the ring.

Thirty minutes pass. Lucy is on her hands and knees looking around and under the bed, while Henry is freaking out, pacing around the room, muttering to himself. With her phone flashlight under the bed, she looks around and sees a glint under the box spring and on top of one of the support beams. She knows that if it *is* the ring, it would be best if *he* were to 'find' it rather than her. Lucy says, "I think I see something down here. Can you take a look?"

He comes to a halt. His eyes bulge, and he quickly dives down to where she is, bumping his head on the bed and almost knocking himself out. She shines the light to highlight the glint. His eyes wide and darting, he looks under the bed and yells, "Yeah! I see something!" He lays face up and squeezes under the bed. His hands disappear under the bed, and after a moment, one hand comes out and presents the ring to her. She lets out a huge sigh of relief.

Exhausted, they both just sit quietly on the floor, seated against the bed, and just decompress. Lucy slowly glances at her watch and quips, "Well, Henry, that's about it for our session today." They look at each other and just laugh.

That evening, she realizes she cannot report what happened in today's session and would have to make something up.

Friday

Dr B reads Lucy's weekly report via email. She describes her treatment with Christina and details her discussions with Henry. She mentions how he writes stories that incorporate the alternate personalities he embodies. Of course, he remains thoroughly skeptical. He shakes his head slowly and thinks, "She's getting fooled by that little twerp. I warned her."

Week 3

Tuesday

Looking for something to act as a catalyst in connecting with Christina, Lucy gets the notion from Henry to bring in some anime figures that she bought at a comic book store. Perhaps it could be something that might trigger Christina to open up. Lucy sets up a figure in the middle of the table. It takes Christina 15 minutes, but she finally focuses on it. Then, after another 10 minutes, Christina *reaches* for it. Lucy is mesmerized. This proves to be a defining moment in her therapy. Lucy is barely able to hold back the flood of emotions she is feeling, sensing a possible breakthrough with Christina. For the remainder of the session, Christina fondles the figure, examining it in detail. Lucy just watches in fascination.

As the session comes to a close, Lucy coaxes Christina to allow her to take it with her. At first, she is reluctant to let go but releases it to Lucy upon gentle persuasion. Lucy would like to have left it with her, but she is not sure of the facility's policy in allowing a patient such as Christina to possess items like this. Christina returns to her blank stare as Lucy assures her that she will bring it back next time. Lucy notices the slightest twitch of a smile, but it fades quickly. As minute as it was, this is significant.

That night, while Jack is snoring away on the living room couch with a ball game on the TV, Lucy is sitting in bed preparing her notes for the following day's session with Henry.

This is when she hatches the plan.

Wednesday

At 9 a.m., Lucy calls PVC and makes up a story about being late so she can see Henry at 12:30 p.m. - to meet Sonya. She uses the old family emergency story.

When Henry is told that Lucy will be arriving later today, he's actually thrilled that he can spend the time writing rather than talking about it. Then he stops, looks up, and, with a grin, thinks, "Hmmm, *Sonya*. Yeah, I think it's about time they met."

After checking in at the front desk, Lucy enters his room at 1:35 and sees Henry already seated at the table with his hands folded. Very cordially, she greets Sonya, "Hello, my name is Lucy… who do I have the pleasure of speaking to?"

"I'm Sonya. Henry's mannerisms and vocal inflections are noticeably feminine. "They told me you are …"

"Lucy… I have been talking with another patient here at the facility."

"That wouldn't happen to be ***Henry***, would it?"

Lucy was intrigued, "Do you know Henry?"

"Yeah, I know him. He's nuts!" spoken like an adolescent girl.

Lucy, astonished, "Nuts? What do you mean?"

"Yeah, you know. He is off his rocker. Wacko; two short-of-a-six pack."

Lucy holds back a laugh, "What, have you met him? Or talked to him?"

"Yeah, once or twice." She pauses to think. "Come to think of it, maybe it was in a dream... or maybe a hallucination. But I *do hear him* occasionally in my head."

Lucy pauses to jot down notes.

Sonya changes the subject and catches Lucy off guard by asking her why she is late.

Lucy stutters but makes up a worthy excuse for her tardiness.

Once they get comfortable with one another's company, Sonya opens up more and turns out to be a very vivacious, talkative teenager. She tells Lucy all about her likes and dislikes. At times, Lucy struggles to get a word in edgewise.

Thursday

When Lucy visits Henry, she then describes her discussion with Sonya.

Henry, grinning, says matter-of-factly, "She thinks I'm crazy, doesn't she?"

"As a matter of fact, yes, she does." They both laugh. "Why would she think that, Henry?"

"I'm like this little voice in their head. I can make suggestions, but I can't interfere with their actions. In Sonya's case, she likes to contend and question the suggestions I make." He proceeds to give several examples of her disagreements.

Henry concludes the topic with, "Next time you talk with her, ask her this for me …… 'Why did you break with Dylan?'" He looks Lucy in the eyes, "I could never understand why she did that. I had trouble writing about it for several days."

Lucy jots down the request, not knowing if she will ever get the chance to honor his request. She gets a contemplative frown and asks, "Did you ever write something contrary to what your Alter did or thought?"

"I try not to, but *yes*, on occasion, I need to make the story work." He says with a chuckle, "So you can say, 'I alter the Alter's story.'"

"Sonya told me that you talk to her in her head… What do you say to the Alters?"

"I'll tell them the story or scene to get their reaction and thoughts on the situation. It's like I'm on the other side of a fence. I can talk, but I can't interfere with their actions."

"So, you are like a director of a movie?"

"I suppose so… if that's what they do."

As the two are wrapping up the session, Lucy asks Henry if she could approach a publisher on his behalf. He contemplates an answer for a long duration. "How does that all work?"

Lucy confesses, "I'm not really sure. This would be my first time with the process myself."

"Do you think people would like my stories?"

Nodding and wide-eyed, "Oh yeah. I *do* believe so," she says confidently.

Lucy asks Henry if she can act as his literary agent. With his permission, she does a video recording of him giving verbal consent.

Friday

That morning, Jack goes to the bathroom to shower and leaves his phone in the bedroom while Lucy is still in bed. It chimes with a message. Thinking it might be Jack's hospital, Lucy picks it up before the security timeout. She finds a text from an "ER – BOH". But it is not what you'd think. Lucy discovers he has been sexting to another woman. She scrolls through the flirtatious texts & sexts. She finds one with a photo with the title "Servicing the cow." This is from the night she discovered him on the phone while they were having sex.

They have a huge blowout. She throws the phone and eventually the engagement ring at Jack. He tries to downplay the situation, which only infuriates her more.

She threatens to call off the engagement and move out. He pleads for reconciliation, but she has her mind made up as she cites his other indiscretions. She leaves the apartment in her pajamas and calls her parents while crying.

Dr. Brown is in his office reading Lucy's latest report. He becomes jealous of Lucy's success with both Christina and Henry. He imagines the embarrassment of a student succeeding in a few weeks when he could not for years. Because of his professional insecurity, he thinks of a way to block her success.

Over the weekend, Lucy goes sobbing to her folk's house, who live in a suburb on the other side of the city. She is welcomed with open arms, and they insist she moves in with them while things smooth over. They try to persuade her to reconcile with Jack, but once she lists all of his indiscretions, they concur he cannot be faithful in marriage and agree with Lucy that the two should call off the engagement.

Over at PVC, it's 8:15 pm, and Henry is Siegfried, an artist from the Mediterranean, who is whimsically doodling in his sketchbook – with amazing draftsmanship.

When she retires for the night, she enters her old bedroom, untouched for five years. There, she indulges in a nostalgic trip while looking at old photos of herself through the years. She focuses on one where she is nine years old with her best friend and neighbor Julianna Ortega - "Julie-O", as she used to call her. The two were BFFs from age four and almost inseparable until Julianna had a traumatic experience that affected her emotionally at age 11. She was institutionalized, and Lucy was devastated by the separation and loss of her best friend. This proved to be the defining catalyst in her life - when she vowed to understand the psychological workings of humans and set the path of her adult life.

Week 4

Monday

In class, Lucy is proud to share and describe her progress with Christina. After Monday morning class, the professor suggested to Lucy to consider becoming an intern at PVC.

Lucy laughs and says, "I don't think that would be a good idea. The thought of working as an underling to Bertrand Brown nauseates me." She says assuredly, "When you get my final report, you will understand why."

Lucy does contact Dr. Brown and gets permission to give Christina one of the anime figures next time. He does give consent, but not without a snotty attitude.

Later that day, Lucy has an initial meeting with a selected publisher and delivers Henry's manuscript for perusal. They arrange for a follow-up meeting the next day.

Tuesday

Lucy greets Christina but only gets a blank stare. When she gets her bag to retrieve the figure, Lucy keeps an eye on Christina's eyes. She sees her glance at the bag. When she pulls the figure out of the bag, Christina focuses on it. Lucy slowly moves it on the table towards Christina, who tracks it closely with her stare. Once at arms-length, she reaches out to it with both hands. She holds it in place and stares at it. After about 15 minutes, Lucy pulls out a second figure while Christina holds her focus on the first figure. Lucy slides the figure behind the first, clearly within her focus. It takes about a minute, but she finally gives a quick glance at the second figure. She looks back at it again and holds her stare on the second. After another 15 minutes, she reaches for the second figure with her left hand, retaining the first with her right.

At the end of their session, Lucy explains to Christina that this is her final meeting with her, not knowing if she understands or not. Lucy then reaches toward the figures, and Christina moves them an inch or two toward herself. Lucy just taps on the figures and says, "Christina, you may keep these." As Lucy gets up and starts walking to the door, she hears the faintest "Thank you" come from Christina. Lucy pauses as her eyes well up, and she says, `You are very welcome'. She wipes a tear from her eye and says a final goodbye to Christina as she exits the room.

Lucy has the second meeting with the publisher, who has a prepared contract ready. They negotiate some minor details before signing. But they insist that next time, the story must be delivered in digital format, as they absorbed the fee for the transcription for this first one. The publisher asks several questions about the author, but she insists that he wishes to be kept anonymous and go with a pen name – to be determined.

Wednesday

Lucy and Henry discuss the upcoming publishing plan and have fun coming up with a pen name for Henry. They decide on Alan Kenneth Ainsworth. Acronym: AKA - their little inside joke.

Henry is telling Lucy about a couple of characters from his latest story when Lucy hears her phone vibrate. She ignores it as she is in session. After several more alerts, she apologizes and excuses herself from the room so she can attend to the messages, as they must be of some importance. She stands in the hallway just outside the room. She reads the message from her mother that Lucy's grandmother has passed away. She was very close with her nana and feels a rush of emotions as she takes a moment to quickly reminiscence. Her late grandfather, who had died a decade earlier, had amassed a fortune with his lucrative stock trades and investments. Lucy later learns she has a substantial inheritance in store for her.

Lucy wipes tears from her eyes and re-enters Henry's room. She apologizes to Henry and resumes, "Where did we leave off?"

He senses something is wrong and instinctively reaches his hand to her upper arm and says "Is everything okay?" He quickly flinches back once he realizes he may have overstepped his bounds by touching her. But she reaches for his hand and holds it when she explains what happened.

That evening, Lucy attends a church memorial service with her parents to mourn the loss of their loved one. Later, when alone in her room, she ponders how this inheritance will enable her to pursue her goals without financial worry. This is when she gets the notion of becoming Henry's legal guardian. She sets up her laptop and begins researching the guardianship process. She even contacts a previous classmate of hers who went into law for his advice.

Thursday

For their final session, Lucy and Henry reviewed the past four weeks and discussed his plans to continue his writing. Lucy makes the proposal to Henry regarding guardianship.

Henry shows strong reluctance to the notion of leaving his familiar situation. "I'm comfortable here…" he says, looking off to the side.

"Henry, you love to write, and you have a very special and wonderful gift. Wouldn't you like to share that with others? I can help you to develop and nurture this extraordinary talent." She crouches close to him and holds his hands. "I don't expect you to make a decision now, but think about it." She leans in and makes eye contact. "I want to help you with your writing. I truly believe this is your calling in life." With glassy eyes, he looks up into her eyes and nods.

The two make plans to keep in touch. As with all the residents, he is allowed to make outside calls on a communal phone in a supervised area. She gives him a card with her cell number on it. "Henry, don't hesitate to give me a call if you need anything or have any questions. If I do not answer, I will call you within 10 minutes after you leave a message."

POST PVC

In her final summary report for class, Lucy describes in detail her experiences and successes with Henry & Christina, along with her brief episode with D'Shawn. However, Lucy berates and derides Dr. Bertrand Brown's professionalism with multiple examples of indiscretion. Later, the teacher meets with her privately and warns her to tread lightly on such accusations as the consequences could be detrimental to her career in the future. "Allegations like that tend to revisit you at a later time." She is given a chance to revise her report and decides this is not the time or place to vent. Instead, she retracts all derogatory statements about Brown and focuses on the patient's progress.

The teacher will also receive an evaluation from the PVC head psychologist, Bertrand Brown, as part of Lucy's final grade. Brown is given one week to submit his report directly to the teacher. Lucy feels apprehensive about what Brown may say as they have had an awkward relationship. She wonders if she has disguised her contempt well enough, or perhaps she may have slipped up at any time.

Lucy gets a two-bedroom apartment downtown in the city. She examines the unit for accommodations, which would include Henry. She looks into the secondary bedroom and imagines his desk and bookshelf setup.

Henry is busy writing away on his latest story – a thriller with a surprise twist ending. He's excited and thinks, "Wait until Lucy reads this one!" He giggles as his puppy-love crush for Lucy has inspired him tremendously and has boosted his confidence. Later, he calls her with the news of his latest story. He also suggests she come to get a previously completed piece to present to the publisher. She informs him she will be making a visit to PVC in a couple of days and will pick up the story then.

Lucy attempts to start up paperwork to release Henry into her care but is stymied because she needs Brown's authorization. Brown blocks the move in his unscrupulous way. He invites her to meet and discuss the matter in his office. He has the audacity to ask, "How much is it worth to you?" as he stands up and unzips his pants.

Lucy calmly says, "I'm recording this entire conversation. Do you want to keep your cushy job and fancy car, or do you want to lose your license over an egregious act of bribery and sexual harassment?"

He is aghast and winces back to his chair while zipping up. After reclaiming his composure, he sheepishly says, "OK, what do you need from me?"

Once he signed over all the necessary paperwork, Lucy concludes with Brown by saying, "When I write about Henry's story, just hope I don't describe you as the douchebag that you really are." She never hears from Brown again.

Before leaving PVC, she stops by to visit Henry to tell him the good news about the guardianship progress. Although she is more excited about the guardianship, Henry is more intent in excitedly describing his latest work in progress. Before leaving, Henry hands over some previously written stories to Lucy to present to the publisher.

A couple of days later, Lucy's teacher lauds her accomplishments after receiving a glowing review and recommendation from Dr. Bertrand Brown. A wide-eyed Lucy holds back her astonishment. Her professor pulls Lucy aside, "Since your initial report, I've heard stories about this Brown. I am now aware of his seedy reputation with women." She looks around and whispers, "You didn't make some 'deal' with this creep, did you?"

"Let's just say the table got turned around on him," she says with a wink.

The teacher, with a knowing grin, "Someday, I want to hear *that whole story*."

"Someday, I'll let you hear the smoking-gun conversation."

Teacher giddy, "Ooh, now you've *really* piqued my curiosity."

The next day, Jack contacts her to get her address, presumably to return some of her items, but she tells him she doesn't need anything left behind and declines to give him her address. He tries for a last-chance reconciliation, but she has prepared for this moment with a laundry list of why that's not gonna happen. She adds with how he blew it, punctuated with "That's the end of it. Period!"

Lucy uses a digitizing service to transcribe Henry's handwritten story he gave her. After proofreading, she submits a PDF to the publishers. They get back to her several days later with approval.

Three months have passed. Lucy succeeds in getting custody of Henry, and he moves into her apartment. She has already prepared a room especially for him with everything he will need - a new laptop with the necessary software and printer. There are bookshelves lining all the walls and a large window looking out over the city on the 22 floor. After giving him a quick tour of the apartment, Lucy goes over a strict set of rules for Henry to follow – principally to keep order, but foremost, for his protection. She has the rules printed on a board so each of Henry's alternative personalities can't miss it.

Despite all of the provisions and instructions on the computer, Henry continues to write in his comp books. Lucy feels frustration but realizes he is not going to change overnight. The transition is a slow process, but he gradually begins using the computer more and more.

Assuming the internet would be an overload to Henry, she allows only the dictionary and Wikipedia to be accessible on the browser. Henry is enthralled by the instantaneous and massive reference material available. For the next week or so, he puts his writing aside and just spends hours going from one hyperlink to the next. During this period, he has one Alter who uses the internet, a male who has bizarre interests, bordering on the maligned - and the internet has plenty of that on hand. Henry sees the red flags with this one and has to persuade an alternative course via suggestion. Henry gets a lesson on how one can focus on the fringe and the bizarre on the web and how this can lead to perversion.

Lucy fosters his talent and helps him bring better control over his personality. Alters by associative techniques. His writing skills blossom as he now is taking advantage of his highly efficient environment with all the tools he needs provided by Lucy. She encourages Henry to set up a schedule to better manage the multitude of Alters he juggles.

Lucy works diligently to get Henry to extend his anchor personality from 90 minutes to 120 – from 11 a.m. to 1 p.m. She realizes this is a delicate matter and treads cautiously through her behavioral modification.

* * *

In the next nine months, Lucy finished her doctoral studies and passed the state licensing exam. She joined a psychiatric group to start her practice. Her new associates give her several patient referrals to get her started.

Lucy accompanies Henry on outside excursions to accustom him to real-life social interactions with the public. These interactions prove valuable experiences for Henry in developing his story characters more quickly and with greater depth. Needless to say, the public experience often has comical, tense, or unnerving consequences – depending on the nature of his present Alter. He may have a polite or rude character manifested. Her supervision during these public exposures is tight or loose, depending on Henry's Alter at the time. His thrill at social interaction leads him to show more affection towards Lucy in the form of increased eye contact and, at times, grabbing and holding her hand. Deep down, Lucy feels a thrill and longing for his contact.

One day, Lucy takes Henry to visit one of the largest and oldest used bookstores in the city. Like a kid in a candy store, Henry is excited by all the books available. She gives him carte blanche to shop, and he has a spending spree. He and Lucy exit the store with arm-loads of books.

By this time, Lucy has been able to interact with 12 of Henry's personalities, most for his new book – a sci-fi/adventure/thriller about a space mission to Alpha Centauri.

One character that was particularly unnerving for Lucy was the adolescent girl who would constantly pop out and try to scare her at any chance she could - it took a while to get used to that Alt. Then there was that one that would masturbate incessantly – that got awkward, indeed. However, Benny was one of Lucy's favorite Alter, as he liked to snuggle and watch movies all the time. Even though she had seen most of them before, she took him through many of those *must-see* movies –the list she calls 'movies to see before you die'.

With Lucy's help, Henry has all his early works digitized to create an anthology of collected short stories. Having already established himself in literary circles, the anthology proved to be a huge success with tremendous sales.

With the income from her practice and her inheritance, Lucy purchases a 2-story brownstone in the downtown area. She plans to use the first story for her practice and the second level for the living area. Lucy announces her plans to break away from the medical group to hang her own shingle.

She establishes and maintains a healthy psychiatric practice from the brownstone. She is able to apply some of the effective techniques used with Henry to treat her DID patients with notable success. Often, the DID patients she would get would be young persons of wealthy parents who kept the child away from the public due to embarrassment. She goes on to write several white papers that are printed in the American Psychological Association Journal.

* * *

Over the next several years, Henry gets four marvelous novels published, achieving both commercial success and critical acclaim. His unique and pervasive character development has garnered across-the-board accolades and recognition. The public gobbles it up, and his books quickly ascend to the New York Times Best Sellers list. AKA is invited to speak at several literary conventions, but Henry and Lucy both concur the time is not yet right and decline the invitations.

They set up the website for AKA and soon sales go out the roof. Soon Alan Ainsworth gained a large following and fan base who wanted to know more about the author. They beg for more disclosure about the author's background, appearance, etc. Lucy discusses this with Henry, but he is quite content with the anonymity and prefers to keep the status quo. He is comfortable with the conducive environment that Lucy has set up for him while maintaining seclusion and privacy.

One day, Lucy receives an exciting call from the publisher informing her that a Hollywood producer is interested in buying the rights to one of Henry's sci-fi stories. When she tells him of the news, he says, "That's a good thing, right?" and goes right back to his writing. She tries not to laugh but just nods exaggeratedly and says, "Yes, Henry. That's a very good thing."

Despite much critical acclaim, not all critics are favorable. Upon reading a particularly derogatory review, Henry is hurt and begins having feelings of inadequacy. Lucy teaches him to constructively handle the detractors and add *recursive learning* to his skill set.

* * *

Zeke

One day, due to a patient cancellation in her schedule, Lucy is done early and decides to finish up some paperwork in her office. It is 4:40 p.m. when Lucy goes upstairs to check on Henry and finds him missing. She calls out for him but gets no answer. After thoroughly checking the house, panic sets in. She even checks hiding places in case there is another adolescent, Alter, who likes hiding. He knows not to go out without her – No. 1 Rule. She maintains herself enough to examine his room and finds notes of the character he last embodied from his schedule. Zeke. A tough guy who takes orders from no one, including Henry - or Lucy, for that matter. All safeguards were violated by this renegade character. She sees that he manifested Zeke 42 minutes ago. Most personalities last for 60 minutes. Her first impulse is to run into the street looking for him. As she frantically looks around, she notices the bus stop, then soon the subway station. Then she gets a gut-punch feeling, realizing he could be anywhere, and begins to fear the worst.

She spends a frantic 15 minutes outside looking around the local area for him. She decides to return to the townhouse and see if he shows up at the top of the hour, which is just a few minutes from now. Upon the no-show, anxiety builds, and she begins calling local hospitals in the proximity. She leaves instructions to seven different hospitals to contact her ASAP if a Henry Taylor or a John Doe is admitted. She downs a sedative to cope with the stress and panic. She admits to herself that she hasn't been monitoring his work as much as she usually does due to her recent workload for her practice and handling the book business. She sits down and begins to read his current story, but the sedative takes over, and she is out like a light with his story in hand.

She is awakened at 1 a.m. by a call from the nearby hospital to inform her of a John Doe admitted to the E/R. With heart racing, her call is transferred to the ICU nursing station. She inquires for details, but the description doesn't match Henry. The huge feeling of relief she feels soon fades to dread, knowing he's still missing. She lets out a deep sigh and tries to calm herself from the adrenalin spike she just experienced. She downs another sedative and dozes off again.

She is awoken by a call at 4:04 am from the downtown UMC to inform her of a John Doe admitted to the ICU. She gasps and loses balance when told of the description. She braces herself not to fall. She takes a quiet moment to collect her senses, then races to the UMC.

She frantically makes it to the ICU to find Henry covered with bandages. He has been restrained with belts. Nurses tell her it is for his own protection because he would phase in and out of consciousness with erratic, sometimes violent reactions.

As she sits and slumps in a waiting-room chair, two police officers introduce themselves to Lucy and describe to her how they came about to find him. In the roughest part of town, a bystander called about witnessing an assault and robbery in progress. By the time the cops arrived, he had been severely beaten and was left for dead. Of course, they ask her, "Why would he even *be* in that part of town?"

After a long sigh, she shakes her head, and she begins to tell them who he is and why he is there.

She successfully persuades them not to leak the story to the media but rather keep it to a single police blotter item of a John Doe.

Doctors examine brain MRIs and decide to perform surgery to reduce swelling in the brain – with Lucy's consent.

She spends all her time there in the ICU – calling her answering service to clear her schedule for the next few weeks. She is so thankful the story didn't reach the news media with his identity and can keep it a private affair. While at the hospital, Lucy can have video chat sessions with a couple of her most vulnerable patients. The hospital staff assisted her by allowing her to use a vacant room for privacy.

She patiently waits to get dialed in with Henry, but it takes days to connect. Several times, Henry becomes conscious, but as an Alter. She becomes depressed with the thought she may never be able to get through to Henry ever again.

On the fourth day, it happens. While she is slightly snoring in the adjacent chair, Henry whispers, "Lucy… Lucy." She rustles in the chair for a different position to sleep. He repeats. She slightly opens her eyes and notices him looking at her. With a crackling voice, she says, "Henry?"

"Lucy, it's me, Henry. "

She throws aside her blanket and lunges to hug him. Weeping, she says, "I thought I had lost you forever." The connection is an immense emotional moment.

Henry is able to explain to Lucy the experience to the best of his recollection. "I was aware of his actions, but Zeke would not listen to the voice of reason when I tried to re-direct him. I was helpless and could only watch when he went on his dangerous way. He wanted to score some drugs, so he went to that seedy part of town, got into an argument, and that's the last thing I remember."

Lucy asks, "Is Zeke still with you?"

"I… I just don't know. My head is in such disarray. I don't know *any* of my Alters. I have no control anymore!" He begins to panic, but she quells his fears with reassurances it will resolve with time & rehab. "I'm so scared, Lucy," he says, sobbing like a little boy in her arms.

She tries to remain by his side 24/7, but the staff urges her to go home and rest.

After 14 days in the ICU, Henry is feeling well enough physically to be released to Lucy and go home.

Henry's convalescence at home lasts for weeks with no sign of personality control, and he is unable to write.

She has difficulty connecting directly with Henry, as he has lost his anchor and grounding base to Henry; she mostly gets various, unrecognizable ALTERS. Alters, such as Benny, Jennifer, and Sebastian – none of whom were in his last story.

He misses a deadline with his publisher, but after she tells them the story – in confidence - they compromise and allow a later delivery deadline for his next book. They are not about to give their cash cow a hard time. However, Lucy is not sure Henry will be able to continue, let alone finish his latest book.

Lucy resumes her practice while Henry stays in his room, circulating amongst his various uncontrollable Alters. Whenever he latches on to his anchor, he notifies Lucy so they can converse.

It was a Thursday when Lucy was in session with one of her clients when she heard a clanking noise from the room above - Henry's room. Lucy tries to stay focused on what her patient Rodney is saying when she hears a rumbling noise above, as if heavy furniture is being moved. She now realizes something peculiar is going on upstairs that she needs to attend to. She apologizes to the client and offers a free makeup session if Rodney can end their session early. He thinks for a moment and says, "Can I get that in writing?" Annoyed, Lucy hurriedly writes on a prescription slip `ONE FREE SESSION', hands it to Rodney, and ushers him to the exit door. She quickly races up the stairs to Henry's room. She knocks but barges in to find him ready to hang himself. He had somehow got an electrical cord looped over a ceiling beam with a makeshift noose on it. He stands on the table, his position moved with his toes over the edge.

He yells, "Lucy, I can't stand it no more! I have no control anymore. I'm finished!" He puts his head in his hands, "I can't write anything!"

Despite her heart racing, she calmly moves towards him while soothing him with words of hope and encouragement. She coaxes him to remove the noose and climb down. They embrace and fall to the floor. She cradles him. They exchange 'I love you' and cry uncontrollably.

The sad moment becomes humorous when Lucy's watch dings to denote the top-of-the-hour, and the next Alter is a hetero female named Alice, who is totally oblivious to the circumstances. Lucy finds herself halfway between laughing and crying when Alice slowly moves away with one of those `what's the matter with you looks'.

Over the next few days, Henry manages to get partial control of his anchor between 11 a.m. and 1 p.m.

A week later, Lucy pops her head to see if Henry is ready. He is dressed nicely in a suit and tie – the first time he has ever worn a suit, so she helps him with the tie. With the smart suit and hair slicked back, he looks like someone out of GQ. Soon, the two are in front of a justice of the peace, reciting their vows. Her parents are the only other witnesses. They had initially shown strong reservations about their daughter marrying Henry, what with the high probability of mental illness to the progeny. But they came to grips with her decision and supported her choice, especially after seeing the extraordinary bond that has developed between the two. It's just as they had always imagined their son-in-law would be a doctor - like Jack.

Their honeymoon was at a fine hotel downtown. Sex is very awkward due to his naiveté. She more or less has to guide him on what to do, plus his hair-trigger makes for brief episodes. However, they soon worked that out. They would rendezvous nearly every day at lunchtime for a tryst. Somehow or another, one day, Henry got a hold of one of those blue pills, causing Lucy to be late for her 1 o'clock session.

With her undying devotion and perseverance, Lucy helps Henry get back his control. They develop new techniques to direct the Alters. One by one, Henry gets control of the Alters once again.

She continues her practice in a limited fashion – by choice. And he went back to his writing. They both collaborate to expunge the Zeke character from his latest story and replace him with a less-troubled character.

Henry finally finishes his book and they submit it to the publishers.

In a year she gives birth to a healthy baby boy, Joshua. Meanwhile, Henry is back to crafting lengthy novels and obtaining critical acclaim. Success and fatherhood, along with the full recovery, have brought newfound confidence in Henry. He discusses it with Lucy, and they decide it is time to disclose AKA's true identity.

After declining for years, Henry and Lucy opt to do book tours and talk-show guest appearances. Of course, timing is everything - all have to be between 11 a.m. and 1:00 pm.

His fan base swells after public appearances and disclosures of events – the M.I.A./Zeke story is a huge draw. They have to deal with the celebrity status with some fans waiting outside their house.

Lucy has to respond to accusations that claim she has *used* Henry for her own gain; she is prepared as she has always considered this accusation would rear its ugly head. She fires back and puts the critics in their place.

Since his recuperation from the brutal assault, Henry had been functioning very well. However, he shows his first signs of memory loss. It starts with simple absent-mindedness but develops into down-right forgetting. He has to deal with the frustration of losing details of his alters.

Lucy eventually closed her practice after effectively treating the last couple of difficult patients to devote more time to Henry and raising Joshua. She begins writing herself.

Joshua grows up accepting his dad's quirkiness and odd behavior. He is accustomed to his dad working in his room most of the time, with an occasional break to interact with him. Lucy monitors Henry's time with Josh.

At times, Lucy will hear profanity coming from Henry's room as his frustration continues to mount due to forgetfulness. His book production suffers.

After 10 years, Henry begins losing control of the 'sundowner Alter'. He even 'loses' a couple of the characters from his current novel – lost to the failing memory that is creeping upon him. By this time Henry's book production fell from two per year to one every other year.

One day, Lucy is cleaning her closet and comes across her old photos. She reminisces about Juliana. Her previous attempts to find her via the internet were fruitless. So she looks up potential private investigators to help see if she can find her. She connects with Stuart Cameron, who specializes in family members and has received very good reviews. After a couple of weeks, Cameron reports that the Ortega family became very wealthy with the father's business. However, to avoid the stigma of shame, they changed Juliana's name and sealed the records. He admits it came to a dead end when Juliana became 21. She just disappeared. Contact with the family was fruitless as they denied her existence and wished to be left alone. Lucy learns to let it go and abandons her search.

* * *

Henry's Death

Dressed in formal, black attire, Lucy sobs and wipes away tears as she sits at Henry's desk. She looks around the room at his notebooks, unfinished works, and the multitude of awards and accolades hanging on the walls. Joshua is now 24 and a pre-med student with strapping good looks in a suit and tie. He pops his head in the door and says, "Mom, we need to go. They're waiting for us." He holds her hand and leads her to the limousine parked out front.

Now seated in the front row at a cathedral, they listen as the minister is giving a eulogy in front of several hundred mourners. At age 56, Henry Parker had passed away from advancing Alzheimer's disease.

Lucy gives a tear-jerking eulogy with an inspirational and uplifting closure. Joshua follows up with an equally inspirational speech, including several humorous antidotes of growing up with his dad.

When receiving condolences after the service, Bertrand Brown shows up. Upon first notice, she seizes up inside, but she relaxes once Brown voices an apologetic and conciliatory speech. She feels a sense of closure knowing that Dr. Brown may have finally grown up and gotten past his perpetual mid-life crisis.

Lucy writes "He DID It" the story of Henry Parker, the DID who learned to control his alternative personalities and write about them to become one of the most significant American writers of the 21st Century.

Having amassed substantial savings from her practice and Henry's royalties, she vows to donate all subsequent proceeds from the Henry Parker royalties and book sales to the research for DID and cure for Alzheimer's disease.

One day, while writing her memoirs, Lucy receives a text. She does a perplexed double-take when she sees the sender. It's from Stuart Cameron, the detective she hired long ago to look for Juliana. It simply reads, "Is this still Lucy?" Frowning, she calls the number, "Stuart?"

Stuart: "Yeah! Lucy! Longtime no talked to. First of all, I'm so sorry to hear about Henry. My condolences. He was an extraordinary person."

"Yes, it was a beautiful service. Henry's legacy will last for a long time. What can I do for you?"

He continues, "Well, you're not going to believe this… *I found her*."

"What?! You found Juliana?"

"Yeah! Juliana, or should I say Julie Olsen. Let me give you some backstory. Since we last talked, I had gotten divorced and my new girlfriend works at the county records. Well, one night, we got pretty smashed, and I guess she wanted to impress me. So she took me to the records department late at night when nobody else was there and I had free reign of the place. And I, well, thought about your case. So, she lets me take a peek at Juliana's sealed record. The parents renamed her *Julie Olsen* and moved her to several different sanitariums. Now, everything that I'm telling you violates the law, so you *have* to keep it strictly confidential. "

With intense focus, "Sure, Stuart, of course!"

"Okay, now, you're NOT going to believe this. Are you sitting down?"

"Yes, yes, go on."

"She was at Pleasant Valley when you met Henry. At the same time!"

Lucy frowns and shakes her head in disbelief.

"Once I found out her new name, I was able to track her. She first went to PVC, then to several other facilities before eventually ending up in some small town in Montana. Do you have a pen and paper? I'll give you the info."

Still stunned, Lucy snaps out of it. "Sure, sure… hold on." She fumbles to grab a pen and writes on the nearest piece of paper. "Go ahead, Stuart" as she begins scribbling down the notes. After writing, she says, "Stuart… *Thank you* so much… What do I owe you for this?"

"Aww, don't worry about it. It's on the house. Just tell me what happens. I'm dying to find out."

After the call, she lets out a sharp sigh. After sitting a while just trying to process the revelation, she calls the Montana small-town facility to confirm the resident Julie Olsen – they are reluctant to say at first, but she uses her credentials to gain privilege, and they confirm her residency there.

Lucy prepares for her journey by packing a couple of bags, and she endearingly places Juliana's photo in her purse. She takes several connecting flights to get to Great Falls, Montana. From there, she gets a car rental to drive 52 miles northwest to a small town called Choteau.

Lucy pulls up to a large, isolated house, obviously converted into a convalescent home. She uses her credentials to gain access to the facility, telling them she had been sent by the family to do a welfare check on Julie Olsen. The staff do not bother to confirm with the family as they have not heard from the next of kin for decades. An attending nurse leads Lucy to the community room, where there are t eight residents. Several are interacting with each other, but the staff member points to a lone, pepper-haired woman in the far corner of the room seated at a small table. She is blankly staring out the window. Lucy's heart is racing as she slowly approaches the sad-looking woman. She pulls a chair up to the table across from her as the woman's focus remains blank and unaware of Lucy. At first, Lucy cannot recognize Juliana, but she soon sees it in her eyes. Lucy's eyes well up, and she holds back from crying. "Julie… Julie Olsen…" No response. "Juliana… Juliana Ortega…." Still no response.

Finally, "Julie-O." Juliana's eyes slowly drift and focus on Lucy's eyes. Once the recognition is made and Juliana's eyes brighten up, Lucy loses it and begins crying for joy uncontrollably. They both begin weeping together as Juliana reaches and clutches Lucy's hands on the tabletop. Lucy places her forehead on their clasped hands.

As they're holding hands and crying, Lucy looks up and leans closely. "We're going to get you well." She wipes away her tears, "And I'm gonna get you out of here." The two stand up to embrace and weep for joy at their reunion - 50 years in the making.

31 Years Ago

In Dr. Bertrand Brown's office at the Pleasant Valley Care psychiatric facility, he is issuing a trainee a third case to interview. He holds up two files, one in each hand, and says, "Eeny, meeny, miny, moe," then holds one up. "Looks like we have...Henry…" When he places the unselected folder back on his desk, the tab reads *Julie Olsen.*

THE END

www.ingramcontent.com/pod-product-compliance
Lightning Source LLC
Chambersburg PA
CBHW040522170726
48295CB00012B/302